Sometimes we find ourselves on a gravel road, not sure of how we got there or where the road leads. Sharp stones pellet the unprotected. And the everyday wear and tear sears more deeply. Saddleback's series, Gravel Road, highlights the talents of our urban street lit authors.

ACKNOWLEDGMENTS

I would like to thank Carson Griffin for sharing her knowledge concerning social services. I would like to thank my children, Sarah, Amy, and Maya, my husband, Tore, and my family for their unending support. Additional thanks to Anne Wanicka, my mentor and friend.

My greatest gratitude goes to my students whose true stories remain more unbelievable than fiction. They are my heroes.

CHAPTER 1

Bad

I wasn't born mean. I hated the word "mean." But being bad was great. It got Mom and Dad to at least look at me. And that's all I wanted.

I started being bad when I was little. Real little, like five. I couldn't figure out why Mom and Dad didn't play with me or touch me anymore. I remember that there had been times before when they did. I thought I had done something to make them stop. So I cried. When that didn't work, I would go up to them and hit. I was reaching for anything.

Mom and Dad didn't do much when I hit them. I wanted them to do something. Even hit me back. They just sat on the couch in a fog of smoke. The smoke made my head spin. I didn't get it then. I get it now. They were so high that they didn't know I was there.

It wasn't always bad with both of them. One time I remember opening the fridge. I wanted something to eat. Anything. There were three things in the fridge. Milk, old cheese that looked green, and one can of soda. I couldn't open the soda, so I started to drink the milk. I put my lips on the jug and tried to drink it. Lumps filled my mouth. I choked a little. Then I spit out a sour mess all over my shirt and the floor. I screamed.

Dad walked in the kitchen. Standing in his boxers he looked at me and cursed. He looked at me. Actually looked at me. "TJ, you clean up that mess!" He threw me a towel, and I cried while I wiped the mess off of me and the floor.

Then I took the towel and threw it at his legs. The white lumps smeared his black legs like paint. I yelled, "I'm hungry!" I stood up and faced the man. "I hate you!" My little hands balled up in fists. I had pulled my shirt off, and I could see my stomach. Spots of white milk stuck to my own dark skin. I didn't care. I was mad. I was hungry.

Dad stared at for me a minute. Then he started to laugh. "Thomas Jahmal Young! You think you can take me?" He ran after me as I took off into the living room, if you could call it that. It had barely enough room for a small couch and TV. He tackled me in front of Mom. She was on the couch and woke up out of a deep sleep. She watched him pin me down. He was laughing. He took his nasty legs and wiped the curds all over my belly. I almost looked white. Then we both started laughing.

"What's going on?" Mom wasn't sure if she should get mad or not.

Dad held me for a moment longer. His grip loosened. I could feel something I hadn't felt in a long time. He rubbed my head and looked at Mom. "Baby, it looks like we need some food." He rubbed my skin. "Our milk has turned into paint."

I giggled. I hadn't giggled much lately.

Mom didn't smile. She turned over on the couch and said, "You go get some. Just leave me alone." Without looking at me she went back to sleep.

CHAPTER 2

The Beginning

School was great. At first. My teachers in kindergarten and first grade thought I was cute. When I'd be rude, they'd laugh. One teacher even said she wished she could take me home. Now I look back and wish she had.

At first I think Mom and Dad were good at getting me to school. They couldn't get me out the door fast enough. Even if I felt sick they made sure I would catch the school bus that stopped at the corner. I only had to walk a few minutes to get there. It wasn't hard since other kids from my building were walking too.

Billy was one of them. He was black too and was a little taller than me. He lived on the first floor, and we would play together on the playground. I would watch Billy hold his mother's hand as they waited for the big, yellow bus to pull up. I wanted to reach out and hold her hand too. I didn't understand why Mom couldn't walk me to the stop, and she told me that holding hands was for babies.

That's when I first started to be mean. At age seven I'd get on the bus and call Billy a baby. "Baby Billy holds Mommy's hand." I would yell until the bus driver made me stop. But it was always too late. Billy would already be crying. He didn't play with me on the playground after that.

CHAPTER 3

Kaden

It didn't take long before Mom bought me an alarm. By third grade she was getting calls from school about how I was starting to miss school. She hated talking to anyone at school. She didn't trust teachers. She always said that they were judging her. They thought they were better than her. I didn't see it. I didn't believe her. I knew that getting up was not something Mom wanted to do. Dad had odd jobs when he wasn't high, so I couldn't count on him. I spent all of third and fourth grade getting myself to school.

I went to school because there was nothing better to do. I wanted to do well. I also loved math. I guess I was good at it. It felt good to see the looks on other kids' faces when they'd see that A on my test. They didn't think a kid like me could get good grades. But my grades really didn't matter to Mom or Dad. So the teacher's threats about getting my homework done didn't bother me. I did well enough on tests. I soon figured they wouldn't fail me even if I never did homework. I made it all the way through eighth grade. I did just what I needed to do and no more.

I had better things to do. I spent little time at home. Mom and Dad didn't care anyway. For a few years I hung around my building. I would start at the playground. It wasn't long before most kids didn't want to play with me. They said I always wanted things my way.

At age thirteen I was bored. That's when I met Kaden Cruz. He was a couple of years older. He was leaning against the fence at the far end of the playground.

"Hey." He smiled at me as I walked toward him. I had never met him, and I had nothing better to do. I thought his cut-off shirt looked cool. His light brown skin boasted a small tattoo. It looked like a band wrapped around his wrist. I couldn't quite see what it was. I didn't want to look too hard. I was afraid he'd get mad. Like it was none of my business.

"Hey." I nodded at him.

"TJ, right?" he asked.

I tried not to look surprised. "Yeah. How'd you know?" I shifted to lean on the fence as well.

"Been watching you." The boy nodded toward the playground. I wasn't sure if that was good or bad, so I just nodded back. There was some silence before he said, "I'm Kaden Cruz." He reached out his hand and I took it. He squeezed it and pulled my shoulder into his shoulder and then backed off again. We looked like two kids trying to be tough. I didn't realize then how tough we really were.

CHAPTER 4

North Side

Do you want to take off?" Kaden looked at me. I paused. I frowned a little, not sure where he wanted to go. As bad as I thought I was, I never really left my street. Kaden nodded at the playground. "Or is there something holding you back?"

I took a look at the kids who were still hanging around the swings. I heard Billy laugh and quickly turned to look at Kaden. I knew those kids didn't want me around. So I shrugged my shoulders trying to look real relaxed. I'd been walking the streets in my neighborhood on the north side of the city a long time. How would this be any different? Still, my heart raced when I answered, "Sure, why not?" I didn't look him in the eye. I didn't want him to see my fear.

We walked down Hillside Avenue for a few blocks. I had passed Thirty-second Street on my own all the time. But it was different when I wasn't leading. We hit Railroad Avenue and turned left. I took a quick look back down my street and could barely see my apartment building. It was lined up with ten other buildings. They looked like huge giants ready to march.

"What?" Kaden's voice broke into my thoughts. "Are you coming?"

I turned to face Railroad Avenue. I knew it wasn't much different than Hillside. On my left, buildings and old houses stood close together. But on my right, the old railroad bed was still showing. Some rusted tracks poked through the dirt and others had been moved. I ran with Kaden across the road to walk along the old railroad bed. We were behind a very large building.

"Hey, it's Walmart!" I said and suddenly felt like a little kid. Kaden just nodded. I added, "I've been in there from the Market Street side." I paused. "Lots of times ... with Dad."

"So?" Kaden didn't stop walking.

"Nothing really. Just have never thought about coming at it from this side." I decided to shut up.

"You'll do lots of things you never thought of ..." Kaden finally smiled. "If you stick with me."

I didn't answer but followed him up the street. We passed behind the bowling alley, and I decided not to point it out. We walked until the railroad bed ended and hit School Road. I started to turn left down the road and guessed we were headed toward North Side Middle School and High School. They were only a couple of blocks down the road. I knew School Road well, so I kept walking.

"Where are you going?" Kaden's voice was behind me. I turned and saw he wasn't leaving Railroad Avenue. He had only wanted to cross the road again. He had stopped in front of an old house. It sat between two other houses that looked just the same. Except for the paint color. It looked like Kaden lived in the yellow one.

I didn't say anything. By the time I caught up with him, he was opening the door. I didn't stop. Not for one second. I walked right on in. The room had a few couches and some posters of hot women on the wall.

"Hey, Kaden. Who's this?" A man about twenty with biceps the size of melons was sitting on a couch. He looked black, but his long dark hair pulled back told me he was part Hispanic.

"Hey, BB." Kaden slapped my back. "This is TJ."

BB kept staring at me. He lifted his arms behind his head and flexed his muscles. I didn't want to look, but I couldn't help it. I noticed he had the same tattoo around his wrist. It looked like a small chain. I suddenly remembered my father telling me about the Hillside Vipers. The gang members wore tattooed chains around their wrists. I realized I may have gotten in over my head. I didn't know what to say, so I just nodded.

I felt a breath on my shoulder. A deep voice whispered, "So you brought us fresh meat?" I thought I would piss in my pants. A tall, white-looking boy with no hair started to squeeze my neck with his hand. I saw the same chain tattooed on his wrist.

"Shut up, Brian!" Kaden shoved him away from me. Brian fell on the couch

next to BB, where they started to laugh.
I thought Brian looked about seventeen.
I took a deep breath and tried to smile. I
wanted to show I could handle a joke.

"Brian and BB like to mess with everyone." Kaden pulled me into the kitchen
and opened the fridge. "You want something to drink?"

"Sure." I was glad to move away from
the laughter.

"Just take what you want." Kaden held
the fridge door open. It was packed. There
was Coke and Pepsi and beer and vodka.
I stood there for a few minutes before
Kaden got mad. "Take something or not!"

I took a Coke, and we walked back
into the other room. I watched Kaden take
a handful of chips from the bag on the
table. So I took some too.

"That's my food!" BB looked serious.

"Thanks!" I said, not knowing what
else to say.

Brian started to laugh. But BB shot him a glance and he stopped. He looked at me again, "So I heard you're a tough guy."

I looked at Kaden and suddenly knew this was all planned. He stared back at me and gave me a "what's your problem" look. I looked back at BB "It depends what you mean by tough." I gulped the Coke down as if I'd never had one before. BB nodded for Brian to get up. He did. He was back in a second and threw a second can of Coke my way. I caught it. Then I smiled, "If it means sitting at home watching TV and drinking what I want all day, I'll be tough!"

They all laughed.

"Yeah! That's it!" BB looked right at me. I knew that was not what he meant. BB knew that too.

CHAPTER 5

Why Now?

Where you been?" Dad stood at the door as I came into the kitchen. It had been a month since I met Kaden, and all we had done was hang at his house after school. Sometimes BB, Brian, and other guys and even girls were there. The most I counted was twenty. Some had names like Bulldog, Snake, or Candy. But most kept their own names. Sometimes they got high or drunk. Sometimes not. Sometimes a few of the guys would disappear upstairs with the girls. Sometimes not.

I was turning fourteen in a couple of days, and the boys told me they had something for me. Summer was coming, and all I could think about was spending more time with them.

"What?" I looked at Dad like he was a stranger. He was sober and his face was serious.

"Where you been?" He stood in the doorway, so I couldn't move into my small room on the other side of the kitchen.

I looked him straight in the eye, "Why do you care?" I tried to shove past him.

He grabbed my arm. "You're my son!" He never took his eyes away from mine.

"Since when?" My words cut. I wanted them to cut. "What? You going to hit me now? You don't have it in you. Why don't you go smoke something!" I pulled my arm away from his grip. Before I turned, I took one last jab, "That's the only way I know you! High and gone!"

Dad followed me to my room. It didn't have a door. It was broken and gone long before we ever moved in. I plopped down on the mattress on the floor. I tried to close my eyes so the man with tears in his eyes would go away. But he didn't.

"You're right." His voice was weak. "You're right." I opened my eyes and frowned. I stared. He continued. "I've seen you with that Cruz boy. You take off with him and do God knows what."

"Nothing, Dad. We do nothing." I sat up and shook my head.

Dad's eyes became hard. "Nothing *yet*."

"What's *that* supposed to mean?" I sneered.

"You'll see." He was calm. "You're with the Hillside Vipers, right? They're feeding you, right?" I just stared, so he continued. "You get what you want, food, movies, and some friends."

"So?" I spat.

"It's not free, son!" He came and sat next to me. "You'll have to pay them back one day."

I frowned. I shook my head, but deep down I knew he was right. I knew it all along.

"Why now?" I asked Dad.

"What?" He looked at me.

"Why do you suddenly care now?" I felt anger well up inside.

Dad just stared at me. He couldn't answer me. He had no excuse. He had no reason. He was who he was. I had to take that moment for what it was. It was mine.

CHAPTER 6

Birthday

Open it!" Kaden yelled above the TV noise. I held the box in my hand. It was an old shoe box. I watched BB and Brian pretend to watch TV. But they would glance at me now and then. I was glad the rest of the gang hadn't showed up yet. Kaden shoved my arm. "Do I got to open it for you?"

"Nah, I got it." I lifted the lid and tried not to frown. I wasn't sure what to think. There was a small package wrapped in brown paper. Next to the package there was a five dollar bill with a joint wrapped inside of it.

BB was looking at me now. He smiled, "The joint's for you! And there's more where that came from." I could feel my face grow warm.

Kaden's voice broke in, "It's a joint man! You know ... pot!"

I looked at him and didn't smile, "I *know* what it is!" All I could see were my parents, high and passed out from drugs. Years of pot smoke already filled my lungs. I wanted to run.

But BB started to frown. "What's your problem? Don't you like it?"

I quickly forced a smile and answered, "Oh, yeah! Can't wait to smoke it." I carefully shoved it in my pocket.

BB smiled. I reached for the other package in the box and started to open it. BB's voice stopped me, "Don't open that!" I looked at him and frowned. He smiled again. But this smile scared me. "That's your first drop off."

"Drop off?" I asked.

"Yeah, drop off ... you take it to a specific place and drop it off." My mind shot to images of drug delivery boys. I had watched them in our neighborhood. I had even seen Dad take packages from one before. I never asked to open his packages. What if it wasn't pot? What if it was meth or a gun? I realized BB was watching me. He kept looking at me straight in the eye. I held his stare. I didn't want him to see my fear. I wanted to be tough. I was tough. I could handle this.

"When?" I felt my jaw tighten.

"Now!" BB looked at Brian and Kaden for a minute and back at me. "The two of them will follow you and make sure you're okay." I wasn't that stupid! I knew okay meant that they were watching out for their package, not me. I just nodded. BB continued, "Go to Got Game Bowling and head to the bathroom. Wait in a stall until someone with red shoes enters the stall next to you. He'll reach down his hand, and you hand off the package."

I didn't move. I just pretended like it was no big deal, "Is that all?"

BB started laughing. "Yeah … go on!"

I stepped out the door and started walking. The back of the bowling alley was only a block down the street, and I would just have to cut around the building to get to the front.

It was already getting dark. I could feel Brian and Kaden following me, but they were far enough behind that they couldn't hear me breathing hard. Once I was in the front of the bowling alley, I walked through the door with neon lights flashing Cold Beer.

I stopped for a minute when I saw the lanes and bright lights. Music filled my body, and I couldn't help smiling. Dad had never taken me bowling. I had heard it was a fun place, but I always called those kids losers. So I made myself think I would hate it. But I didn't. The smell of fries made my stomach growl. I glanced at the counter where it looked like a hundred shoes were lined up. A tall white man, who looked like he had just stepped out of an army poster, looked at me.

"What can I do for you?" His voice was strong and his eyes narrowed.

I could suddenly feel myself sweat. "Oh, I just need to use the restroom." I tried to smile.

"Customers only!" The army man's strong hand pointed at a sign.

I panicked, but only for a minute. "Oh." I shifted. Then I pointed at the fries. "How much are they?"

"Two bucks." The man turned his head and handed a young girl and her father some shoes.

I walked up to the bar and sat down. I put the package on my lap and ordered some fries and a Coke. I carefully pulled the five dollar bill out of my jeans leaving the joint hidden. I knew then why BB gave me the money.

I ate slowly. I enjoyed the fries and the cold Coke. The drink suddenly gave me a real need to use the restroom.

The restroom was small with two stalls. I picked one and closed the door. I decided to wait until the red shoes arrived before I actually used the toilet. But after fifteen minutes, I was dying. I put the package on the back of the toilet and unzipped my pants. Just as I was finishing, I saw the red shoes. I panicked and tried to grab the package. But it slipped. It fell into the toilet. My heart stopped. I stood and looked at the package floating in my piss. I cussed and grabbed it. I used toilet paper to wipe it off, but it did no good. I slowly handed a wet package to the dark hand that belonged to the red shoes.

I held my breath as curse words flew from the stall next door. I didn't dare move. Suddenly there was a roar of laughter. I recognized BB's voice and opened the door to find all three of my new friends laughing.

I didn't feel like laughing, but I tried to smile. "What's going on?"

Kaden spoke first. "You really dropped it in the toilet?"

"I didn't mean to." I tried to laugh, but I know I sounded fake.

BB threw the package in the trash and looked at me. I was confused. He smiled. "It was just some old paper. We wanted to see what you would do." His eyes narrowed and his smile was gone. "Next time it will be for real. Just don't take a piss first!"

They all started laughing again. I swallowed hard. Next time. I wasn't sure I wanted a next time.

CHAPTER 7

Alone

I held the joint in my hand as I sat on my bed. It was only four in the afternoon, and I was home. I had spent the last week of school running home from the bus stop. I didn't want to face BB again. I thought I was tough, but I didn't want to be. Teasing and acting mean to kids on the block was one thing. Delivering drugs was something else. I was too afraid. I hated myself for it. I believed I was weak. I believed I was worthless. I couldn't even smoke my birthday gift. I didn't want to.

I heard a dish fall in the kitchen. I stood up quickly and stepped out of my room. I saw Dad stumbling around the table. I thought he was drunk or high again, so I stepped right back into my room. Then I heard a thud. I knew he must have hit the floor hard. I leaned back on my bed up against the wall. I was waiting for his usual snoring. But it didn't come. I lifted my head and listened. It was quiet.

I shot out of my room and was leaning over Dad. His eyes were open but he wasn't breathing. I started screaming and shaking him.

"What's going on?" Mom stood in the opening to the living room. Her hair was pressed up to one side of her head. She was only wearing a bra and sweat pants.

I was still shaking Dad. I screamed, "He's dead. I think he's dead." Tears made it hard for me to see.

I felt Mom shove me out of the way. "Oh no! *No*!" She screamed. She turned and looked at me with fear in her eyes. She yelled, "Call nine-one-one!"

I started patting down Dad. Each pat felt like I was touching a strange mass lying in the middle of the kitchen. I finally reached for Dad's jean's pocket. I had to shove him on his side so I could pull out his cell phone. I dialed.

Thirty minutes later the police found us still sitting beside Dad. But we were just sitting next to a dead body. Mom had her head between her knees and was rocking back and forth. I was just staring. I knew the minute they came in that more than Dad would be taken away from me. They would find the drugs still cluttering up the living room. They would find the small amount of pot in my room. I knew nothing would be the same.

The police called it Protective Services. They took me. Away from my neighborhood. Away from my mother. Away from everything I knew.

I was alone.

CHAPTER 8

South Side

They told me I wouldn't leave the city. But it felt like I did. They took me to the south side of town. "It will be good for you to spend some time away." Miss Miller tried to smile at me from the driver's seat. A trash bag with a few of my things was thrown in the back seat. She was young, maybe twenty-five. If I hadn't been upset or angry, I would have thought Miss Miller was hot. But I didn't care that her long, dark legs looked like they'd walked right out of one of the posters hanging in Kaden's house. She had tight corn rows, and she tried to look older by wearing a suit jacket. The air conditioning was blasting to help keep that jacket on.

"Whatever," I whispered and leaned my head against the window.

"TJ." Miss Miller was really trying. "You won't be at Miss Dixie's forever. Once your mother takes some classes and gets the help she needs, she can get you back."

I turned my head to stare at her. I gave her the coldest stare I had. "Just shut up. You don't know me, and you don't know my mom. She'll leave me to rot." I turned my head and leaned against the window again.

I think she said more things, but I didn't listen. I let her voice drift away. I watched the tall buildings of downtown pass by. The people on the sidewalks looked like they were dancing around each other but never touching. Soon the busy downtown gave way to neighborhoods a lot like mine. After a few more blocks, we finally turned into Grant Park. The streets were lined with houses and some apartment buildings. But they were all facing a wide open green space in the middle. I found myself looking at a small pond with a bridge over it. A girl about my age was sitting on its edge. Her white legs and short red hair made her stand out against the wooden bridge. I couldn't help but stare. I hadn't seen many redheads.

"We're here." Miss Miller touched my shoulder. But I quickly jerked away from her touch.

"Don't touch me," I said as I looked away from the girl.

Miss Miller just nodded. "Isn't this nice?"

Across from the pond there was a brick house, larger than Kaden's, and it had a porch with a hanging swing.

I just sat in the car and watched Miss Miller go to the front door. It only took a minute before a huge black lady came to the door. Her hair was sticking out all over the place. She was patting it down with both her hands until it lay flat ... sort of. Her smile was so big I swear I could see all her teeth. She waddled as she walked toward me. Miss Miller waved at me to get out. I didn't at first. But something about the big woman's smile made me slowly get out of the car. Once I slammed the door behind me, I just stood there. I put my hands in my pockets.

"This is Miss Dixie." Miss Miller pointed at the woman like I couldn't see her.

Before I knew it, the biggest arms pulled me into the biggest breasts I had ever seen. My hands were stuck in my pockets. But it didn't matter. I was too shocked to push away.

CHAPTER 9

Miss Dixie

This'll be your room, TJ." Miss Dixie was out of breath. We had only walked to the second floor. I could see there was one more flight of stairs. Large arms opened the first door at the top of the steps.

Miss Miller was standing behind me. "Go on in, TJ." I turned and glared at her. She did nothing but piss me off. So I didn't move. I sucked air between my teeth, so she would know I wasn't doing anything she said.

"Oh, Patty," Miss Dixie took Miss Miller's arm. "Let's leave TJ alone and just give him some time. Why don't you come on down for some sweet tea?"

"But …" Miss Miller began to protest.

"I won't take no for an answer." Miss Dixie was practically pulling the skinny woman away from me.

I waited until they were gone before I turned to look at my room. I touched the door. I'd never had a door to my room. Then I frowned. But it wasn't really mine.

I stood in the doorway and saw a bed sitting up off the floor. It already had a blue blanket spread across it, and two pillows sat neatly at the head. A small desk with a lamp was next to the bed. I could see the lamp would work for the desk and the bed. A picture of some mountain was hanging above the desk. A small closet was on the other side of the bed. I wondered what I'd put in the closet since I was only holding a trash

bag with a few shirts, pants, and a handful of underwear.

"I have the same room." A voice
broke into my thoughts. I turned to see
the redhead from the bridge looking into
my room. She didn't look at me. She just
stared into the room. "But mine has a
green blanket and a picture of a lake. Wish
I knew where the lake was. Would like
to go there someday." Then she looked at
me. Her eyes were so blue that I stared
into them a second too long. She smiled
for just a second, and then she turned and
headed up the stairs. I could hear a door
close right above me.

I stared after the girl for a minute
thinking I must have landed in a nut house.
Never had any white girl just talked to me
like that. And I wasn't sure what *that* was
about. At school there were a few white
girls. But they would either flirt with me or
stay clear of me.

I finally walked into my room. I threw the bag into the closet and fell down on the bed. There was a window next to the bed. I could see the pond and the houses. They surrounded Grant Park like a small fort.

"So how do you like it?" Miss Dixie was in my doorway. I had forgotten to close the door. Something I needed to start doing. Now that I had one.

"Okay I guess." I looked out the window again. I soon felt the weight of someone sitting down on the foot of my bed. I quickly pulled my legs up to my chest. Miss Dixie was sitting so close to me. It freaked me out just a little. "What do you want?" I didn't try to sound mean. But it still came out that way.

Miss Dixie smiled. "TJ, I just want to rest, son. You see how many times I went up those stairs in the last twenty minutes? I think I deserve a sit down." She raised her eyebrows. "Don't you?"

I stared at her and saw a single drop of sweat fall down her cheek. "I guess so," I said, not really knowing what to say.

"TJ." She looked at me with the same smile. But there was a serious look in her eyes. "I know this is not home. I don't expect it to be. But maybe," she paused and reached out for a quick pat on my leg, "maybe you can think of this as your sit-down time." I frowned slightly. She continued, "I think you need it."

"What do you know of what I need?" My anger was rising, and I pulled my legs in even closer. I could hardly breathe.

Miss Dixie didn't answer. She just stood up and took a deep breath. "Ah, I feel better already." She looked at me and smiled. "Thank you for letting me rest." She began to walk out my door. She spoke without looking back. "Wash up. Dinner is in ten minutes."

CHAPTER 10

Dinner

I know it sounds crazy, but I had never been "called to dinner" before. Sure, once in a while Mom or Dad had told me if I wanted something to eat to grab it. But I was lucky when there *was* something to grab besides cold pizza or cereal.

Telling me to wash up and join Miss Dixie for dinner was like telling me to tie my shoes for the first time. I awkwardly found the bathroom next door and washed my hands. Twice, just in case. Then I headed down the stairs. I didn't hear Miss Miller's voice anymore, but I wasn't sure she was gone. I slowly looked around the corner. I walked through a large living room with a couple of couches and a big TV. The living room carpet on the floor ended. The beginning of wood floors was the only way you knew you were in the kitchen. There was no wall between them.

The large kitchen had a long table set for six. One end of the table was shoved up against the wall, giving Miss Dixie more room to move between the fridge and the sink. I walked up close to the fridge and was shocked at its size. I thought I heard something and quickly looked behind me. But it was nothing.

"Don't worry. She's gone." Miss Dixie smiled at me. She was near the sink. "I sent Miss Miller home as soon as I could." She handed me a bowl of mashed potatoes. "Please set this on the table." I held the warm bowl for a minute and then looked at her awkwardly. "Go on. Put it down anywhere." She turned back to the oven and pulled out some baked chicken.

My stomach growled. It hurt so bad. I couldn't help but feel some excitement about sitting at this table. Even if I didn't know who would be sitting with me. I carefully placed the potatoes near the middle, next to some warm rolls.

"Dinner!" Miss Dixie's voice yelled so loud that I jumped. She giggled and said, "Sorry, next time I'll warn you that I'm calling everyone."

Soon I heard footsteps crashing down the stairs. A small Hispanic boy came charging in the kitchen and headed straight for the chair nearest to me. He looked about eight. He stopped for one second and looked at me. He frowned a little and then smiled. "You must be new."

"You think?" I said.

"Whatever," the boy said. He didn't care if I was rude or not. He looked at the food and yelled as loud as he could. "She said dinner!"

"Now, Rico! No need for both of us to scream. They're probably washing their hands." She smiled at him. "Did you?"

Rico sighed and ran to the kitchen sink. He washed for a second before running back to his seat. As I was watching this, I felt a small hand touch mine. I jerked my hand away and looked down to find a small, blond girl looking up at me. Her hair was held back in a pony tail by a huge red bow. "Hi, I'm Mae. I'm four. Will you sit next to me?" She reached for my hand again. I didn't know what to do, so I let her hold it. But I didn't really hold her hand. My hand was as stiff as a board. She didn't seem to care. Mae pulled me to the seat across from Rico and next to her. The living room was behind us.

I looked at Miss Dixie who nodded. "That'll be a fine seat for you TJ."

"Oh, what a funny name." Mae let go of my hand and giggled. "TJ, TJ, TJ," she repeated.

"Shut up!" I said to the little girl. Her smile turned upside down. Big tears started to fall down her chubby cheek. I stared. I wasn't sure why she was crying.

"We don't say *shut up* to each other TJ," Miss Dixie said. But she was just stating a fact. She walked over to Mae and patted her once on the head. "Mae, you can pull your smile back up. TJ is new and doesn't know how it works here."

Mae's frown disappeared as fast as it came. She looked at me and smiled. "Okay. I forgive you TJ."

I could feel a heat rise in me. What kind of place was this? I hadn't done anything wrong, and they were already making me look like I was stupid. I felt myself wanting to take off. But just then Miss Dixie put the baked chicken down in front of me. Leaving could wait until later.

As I stared at the chicken, I felt myself reach for a piece. "Got to wait till we're all seated," Mae told me. I put down my hand and stared at the blond brat next to me.

Just then a tall, thin black kid walked in. He had glasses on and his hair was cut short. He sat down between Rico and the wall. He briefly looked at me and nodded. I nodded back.

"That's Prince," Mae whispered. "He don't talk much."

I looked at Prince who didn't seem to care he was just being talked about.

"Hi again. I'm Annabelle." The red-head plopped down next to me. "I see you are sitting on the girls' side."

Mae and Rico laughed. Prince didn't care.

"Miss Dixie put me here." I felt my face get hot again. Now I'm a girl?

"Chill!" The girl gently touched my arm. "I'm just teasing."

"I'm hungry!" Rico protested.

"Okay, everyone hold hands." Miss Dixie smiled as she sat at the end of the table. I looked around the table and saw everyone willingly reach out for each other. Even Prince.

I felt Mae's hand again, and I looked awkwardly at Annabelle. She smiled and whispered, "Don't worry, I washed." She held out her hand. I watched my dark hand being gently folded into her soft white hand.

I watched Miss Dixie close her eyes and say, "God bless the food. Amen!" As soon as she opened her eyes the new strange group of people ate. And I ate.

CHAPTER 11

Annabelle

So you want to go to the bridge before it gets too hot?" Annabelle had shoved open my door. I was still in bed. I cussed and threw my covers up over my bare chest.

"What do you think you're doing? My door was closed." I sat up and stared at the girl.

She had on blue shorts and a skimpy tank top. She just leaned against the doorway with her arms crossed. "Well, it seems to me you need someone to show you the neighborhood." She just stood there. "Well, are you coming or not?"

I couldn't believe it. I took the covers and turned my back to her. "Not!"

Before I knew it, Annabelle had grabbed my covers and started jerking them off me. Her laughing voice never changed. "Come on sleepy head! Get up!"

I jumped up and stood there facing her with only my boxers on. I was so mad. "What kind of freak are you?" She stood there with the covers in her hand looking at me. Her smile was gone. I could smell the strawberry lip gloss she had smeared awkwardly on her lips. I grabbed my covers away from her and threw them back on the bed. I started yelling, "What kind of place is this?"

"But I was just …" Annabelle started.

I wasn't finished. "You were just what? *Freak*! Trying to see me with my clothes off? There you go, take a good look!" I held my hands above my head and turned once around for her. "So do you like see-ing a black man half naked?" I walked in close to her. I flexed my right arm up in her face.

I had gone too far. Annabelle's face was red. Tears were falling. But she made no sound. She was shaking. Her eyes were no longer looking at me. They held a gaze I did not understand.

I dropped my arm and stared. One more cuss word fell from my lips as I watched a small puddle form at Anna-belle's feet. I couldn't believe she had just pissed on my floor.

"Oh my Lord," Miss Dixie came run-ning into the room. She had a serious look on her face as she saw me standing there in my boxers. "I thought I heard some yelling." She gently touched Annabelle's arm. "Annabelle, honey. It's Momma." An-nabelle slowly turned her head and looked at the large woman next to her. Annabelle nodded and reached out to bury her face in Miss Dixie's arms. "There, there child. Momma's got you." She moved Annabelle out of my room and up the stairs.

I crawled onto my bed and stared at the small puddle on the floor. I wasn't touching it. I could hear the shower running in the upstairs bathroom and then more soothing sounds from Miss Dixie.

It felt like forever, but Miss Dixie did come back to my room with a bucket. She got down on all fours and scrubbed my floor. I stared. I had never seen such a large woman get down that low. Using the edge of my bed, she pulled herself back up.

Then she looked at me. She didn't look angry. But her softness was gone too. "TJ this may not be your home. You may not be here long." Her eyes narrowed. "But remember, some of my kids will never go home. And Annabelle is one of those. I'm her momma now." A tear fell down her cheek. She didn't try to hide it. Her large hand slowly reached up to wipe it away. Miss Dixie sighed. "I don't know everything you've been through. But you're not the only one who's been hurt." She turned to go.

I felt my stomach turn. I felt like I had done something awful. I felt like I had hurt Annabelle. But anger soon reached my lips. "I didn't do anything wrong! She came into my room! It's her fault!" I whined.

Miss Dixie turned to look at me. A gentle smile returned to her eyes. "I never said you did anything wrong. Annabelle should never have come into your room." She paused and took a deep breath. "She was just trying to be your friend."

CHAPTER 12

Summer

Annabelle stopped talking to me. Mae didn't. It didn't seem to matter how many times I tried to get the little girl to leave me alone. She would come back and keep talking to me. So I spent a lot of time in my room.

Rico played with the neighborhood kids all day long. I'd look out my window and watch him take his bike and ride up and down the streets. There were about four white boys who rode with him. Sometimes they'd swim in the muddy pond. Sometimes I wouldn't see him until dinner. Dinner was spent most evenings with

Mae and Rico talking about their day. Prince kept to himself. I found it strange how he was able to take off on his own some days.

Miss Dixie took us on small trips, but I could tell she hated it. The heat really got to her.

I'd been to the zoo before with my school. The trip with Miss Dixie was different. I didn't care too much about the animals. I kept looking around to see if there was anyone there from my old school. Before I knew it, overheated Miss Dixie piled us up into her van. We headed home.

Miss Dixie much preferred taking us to the pool. It was only a few blocks away. Rico and Mae loved it. Miss Dixie did too. She and Prince sat at a small table in the shade and watched us as they drank cold lemonade.

"TJ, will you be so kind as to keep an eye on Mae?" Miss Dixie asked as I headed toward her to sit as well. I hadn't planned on swimming either. I couldn't swim. But I wasn't telling anyone.

"I just want to chill." I sat down next to Prince.

"Oh, I guess you're tired too." Miss Dixie started to get up. I looked at Prince, and he stared at me. He didn't have to use words but his eyes screamed, *Are you crazy? Making this woman get up and stand out in the heat!* I rolled my eyes at him and then stood up.

"Okay, Miss Dixie. I'll watch Mae." I was walking away from the table but then turned to ask, "What am I watching her for?"

Miss Dixie was smiling, "Oh, she can't swim. So just make sure she comes up again if she goes under water."

"Oh, great!" I whispered to myself and shook my head.

I stood next to Mae in the kiddie pool. The cool water did feel good on my feet. I was as close to Mae as I could get. When she moved closer to some other kids, I moved too. A couple of white mothers were tanning. When they saw me towering over Mae, they started whispering. Soon they were in the water with their own kids. But they still looked at me. I glared at them a couple of times. I crossed my arms and wasn't going to move.

As time passed I found out Mae wasn't going to drown. So I looked around a little more. I saw a redhead at the far end of the diving pool. Annabelle was sitting on the edge. Even from where I was I could see her sun lotion was so thick she looked like she'd been painted white. For one moment I felt myself smile. I remembered my father. I remembered the few moments of closeness. I remembered white milk curds covering my stomach. My eyes suddenly blurred. I had to find a way to push the thoughts away. I wasn't going to cry. Not there. Not then.

I swung my leg and splashed Mae. She looked up at me with water dripping down her hair. "TJ. Oh, you'll get it now!" She took her little arms and started splashing me. All the little kids joined in. I pretended to fall into the water. I let the water mask the flow of my tears.

CHAPTER 13

August

I told myself I was happy without Annabelle bugging me. But sitting next to her at dinner with her never looking at me felt weird. She didn't hold my hand for the prayer. Miss Dixie didn't make her. I thought Annabelle would shake it off. But she didn't.

Miss Miller came by once in a while to check on me and let me know Mom was not making much progress. This was never a surprise to me.

As the summer and long days passed by, I realized that I was going to be at Miss Dixie's for the long haul. This meant I would go to South High in the middle of August. I wasn't happy about this. I had looked forward to my high school years at North High. I was already a top dog. Nobody would mess with me. Now I would have to prove myself all over again.

It was early August. I leaned against my window and saw Annabelle on the bridge. It was her favorite spot. I realized that I never saw her with other girls. She wasn't like Rico. She didn't make friends easily. Maybe we had something in common after all. I took a deep breath and headed out of my room.

"Hey." I stood far enough away from her so that I wouldn't scare her. She looked at me and then looked back at the water below her. "What's up?" She didn't answer. So I tried again. "Can I sit?" She still didn't move and didn't answer. "I take that as a yes, since you didn't say no." I sat down near her and let my feet dangle too. I could smell her strawberry lip gloss and smiled. I knew right away why she loved this spot. You felt for just a minute like you were somewhere else. The trees along the park hid a lot of the buildings, and grass spread out on both sides of you. I had never seen so much green in my life. "Wow! Great place!"

Annabelle looked into the water. She let her legs move slowly back and forth.

"Look, Annabelle," I said, feeling like I was doing something that wasn't me. "I didn't mean to hurt you." She was quiet and her legs stopped moving. "I mean, you really freaked me out, girl." I tried to smile. "Think about it. What would you have done if some black boy came into your room and started pulling your covers off?"

She suddenly turned her head and looked at me. Her blue eyes met mine. She held me with her look. I couldn't tell if she was about to freak out again or laugh. She was thinking.

"I never thought of it that way." She kept looking at me. She was so intense. I wanted to look away, but I didn't. She finally said, "I guess I would have hit you." A small smile started to appear. "Thanks for not hitting me." She turned to face the water again and her legs started to swing.

"You're welcome, I guess." I said, wondering what had just happened. In a sort of weird way, we had moved on.

"You see that tree over there?" Annabelle pointed at a huge pine tree. It looked like the biggest Christmas tree I had ever seen.

"Yeah," I answered.

Annabelle slowly pushed her hair behind one ear. "I dream on it."

I frowned a little. "What? You dream on it? What the heck does that mean?" She looked at me with a frown. I smiled. "Just asking—not being mean—I promise."

Her smile returned. She took a deep breath. "I dream one day I will have a house with a big tree like that. Maybe it will be near that lake in the picture on my wall."

I looked at the tree and only saw a tree. Still I wanted to say something. "Some dream!"

She looked at me and her eyes held me again. "What's your dream TJ?"

I felt stupid. I shifted. I looked up to the sky. I leaned back on my arms. I finally answered, "No idea. Never had a dream. Just want to live I guess." I looked at her and she was still staring at me. "Does that count as a dream?"

She smiled. "I think it does."

During the prayer at dinner that night, Annabelle held my hand. I held it back.

CHAPTER 14

South High

South High seemed okay. Miss Dixie made sure Annabelle and I had all our freshman classes together. I wasn't sure why she did that. I didn't need a baby-sitter. I soon realized it wasn't for my sake.

We were in the hall putting our books in the lockers. My locker was across the hall from hers. I threw my books in it and slammed the metal door shut. I turned to face Annabelle to see if she was ready to head off to math, but she was taking her time. So I decided to lean against my locker.

"Hi, Annabelle." The hottest girl I'd ever seen walked up behind Annabelle.

The girl's long, black hair was perfectly straight. It fell softly over curves that made my insides hurt. It looked like she'd spent the summer tanning, so her skin was almost as dark as mine. I was excited that Annabelle had a hot friend.

Annabelle turned and smiled, "Hi, Rani." I could see Annabelle was a little nervous. Rani flipped her hair back and spoke to some girls that came up behind her. They giggled. The group all looked like they'd bought clothes at the same place. I knew then Rani was not her friend. Annabelle turned to finish closing her locker.

"I wasn't done talking to you." Rani's voice changed. "I can't believe you actually made it to high school." She didn't look so hot anymore. The other girls were laughing, and a small crowd started to form.

"Rani, I need to go ..." Annabelle whispered.

"*Go* is right." Rani laughed. "Like *go* in your pants." Annabelle's eye's dropped to the floor. Rani started to grab Annabelle's shorts and pull on them, "Or are you wearing diapers?"

"Back off!" A strong voice shut Rani up. I wished it had been mine. But it wasn't. It was Prince. He was up in Rani's face, "I don't ever want to hear you mess with Annabelle again! You may have gotten away with it in middle school but not here!"

Rani lifted her chin. "Who are you?" She tried to smile at him. A sick flirt. "Look here, beautiful black man, I've got way more to offer you than this girl." She tried to touch his arm, but he backed up. Annabelle was hiding behind him. She was holding onto his shirt. He was the wall between Annabelle and the ugly world.

"Shut up!" Prince said. He looked Rani in the eye and spoke without missing a beat. "Annabelle is my sister. If you mess with her, you mess with me." Rani shut her mouth and swallowed.

Prince turned and wrapped his arm around Annabelle's shoulder. I heard him whisper, "I'll walk you to class. Don't worry about it. They'll leave you alone."

Annabelle tried to smile. She looked back at the girls standing in the hall in shock. She looked at Prince and answered, "Okay, Prince, I believe you."

Rani saw me staring and hissed, "What *you* looking at?"

I gave her my best mean look, cussed, and spat, "Not much!" I turned and ignored the words she was throwing at me down the hall. "Better me," I thought, "than Annabelle."

When I reached the classroom, Prince was coming out of the door. I stopped as he grabbed my shoulder. He pushed me up against the wall and spoke his first words to me, "Who *are* you?"

"What?" I was trying to push him away, but he was stronger.

"Who are you?" Prince repeated. He was so close I could smell the morning coffee on his breath.

"Come on, Prince. Put me down. I don't know what you're talking about." I was trying to be calm but anger was starting to rise. I could see other kids starting to stand around, waiting for a fight.

"What's going on out there?" A teacher's voice came from somewhere.

Prince loosened his grip. But he was still up against me. "Were you just going to watch that girl make Annabelle piss in her pants? Do you really not care?" His eyes were full of disgust. He pointed into the classroom. "You watch out for her. If you don't, I will never let you forget it."

I knew then that I was the baby-sitter. Whether I liked it or not.

CHAPTER 15

Prince

Prince was a senior. After that first day we didn't see him much at school. I was surprised to see he had some friends. He actually looked like he was talking to them. I didn't get Prince. I thought he was a freak. But then I started wondering if he just didn't talk to me because he didn't like me. I guessed after that first day of school I was right. He thought I was nobody. That's who I was.

It took me about a week to knock on Prince's door. I'd never been into his room. I didn't know anything about him.

"Who is it?" Prince's voice sounded like he'd been asleep.

"It's TJ." I paused and then added, "Never mind. Sorry to wake you." I turned to go when Prince open the door. His shirt was off and his room was dark.

He nodded for me to come on in as he walked over to the window. As he opened his blinds, afternoon light spilled into the room. He sat on his bed and reached for his glasses. I just stood there. His room was different than mine. It was bigger and there were posters everywhere. His closet had clothes pouring out of the door. His desk had a pile of books and a computer. He even had a small TV near his bed.

"What?" He asked as he watched me scan his room.

"Wow. You must have been here a while," I said.

"My whole life." Prince took a deep breath.

"Miss Dixie took you in when you were a baby?" I was confused.

"Nope." Prince smiled just a bit. "Miss Dixie gave birth to me. She's my mother."

Suddenly it all made sense. This was Prince's house, and I was just another kid passing though. He called Annabelle his sister because she was. Miss Dixie had said Annabelle was never leaving. They were a family. I was an outsider. I looked at him. "You know I didn't ask to come here." Prince just stared at me like this was nothing new. His eyes told me he sure wasn't feeling sorry for me. I turned to go.

"That's it?" Prince asked. "You woke me to tell me that?" He shook his head. "TJ, you are pretty messed up."

"I'm messed up?" I spun around and anger shot through my words. "I'm messed up?" I was shaking now. "I'll tell you what's messed up. This place is messed up!"

Before I could continue, Prince jumped out of bed and was up in my face again. "What? Are you saying it's messed up here because you get a home-cooked meal every day. A little four-year-old girl loves you for no good reason. My momma treats you like you were her son. And a redhead feels like you're her only friend. Yeah, sounds messed up, TJ." He pushed me out the door and slammed it. I could hear him blast some music, so he wouldn't have to hear me yelling back.

I guess Prince still thought I was nobody.

CHAPTER 16

Lunch

I found myself in a weird place at school. I was new. Even though it was a big school, some kids tried to get to know me. I would look at them like they were stupid, and then they'd leave me alone.

"Why do you do that?" Annabelle asked me at lunch. We were sitting together eating pizza.

I took a drink of my small chocolate milk and looked at her. "What do you mean?"

"Why do you push all the nice kids away?" she asked. Her blue eyes were looking at me like she had just asked me why I was drinking chocolate milk instead of orange juice.

"What are you talking about?" I took a bite of the pizza.

Annabelle took a napkin and pushed it down on her pizza. Grease soon turned the napkin orange. After she had used a pile of napkins she took a bite and looked at me again as she chewed. "You know what I'm talking about. I've seen you be mean to nice people. You make them afraid of you. Like you don't like anyone." I shrugged my shoulders. She continued, "You know, you could be here a while. You need to have some friends."

I took another bite and looked at her. "But I've got you."

Annabelle stopped chewing and her face turned red. She smiled. "Yeah, I know." Then she looked at me again, "But you can't go on being mean."

I frowned just a little. "I'm not really mean." I hated that word. Rani was mean. I was just tough. "I only want them to leave me alone."

"But why?" Annabelle took another bite.

I paused and thought just a minute. "Because that's the only thing I know how to do."

"Well Mr. TJ, you're very good at it." Annabelle smiled and had pizza all stuck up in her teeth.

I laughed. I couldn't remember the last time I laughed.

"What about you?" I asked.

Annabelle frowned. "What about me?"

I tried to keep it light. "Well, you asked why I chase people away. I don't see you talking to a lot of kids." I finished off my chocolate milk.

"They don't talk to me," She said as she started folding her napkins. The grease painted her fingers orange.

"Why?" I handed her my clean napkin. She took it and wiped her fingers. Then she folded that napkin and placed it on top of the others.

"Because they think I'm weird." She looked at me. I looked at her perfectly stacked napkins.

I smiled. "Look normal to me."

Annabelle smiled back. "You're just saying that to be nice."

I threw my hands in the air and joked, "One minute you call me mean and the next minute nice. So which is it?"

She never answered my question. But her eyes did. At that moment there was something about her look that scared me. In a good way. Like I wanted to keep looking. But if I did, I would lose a part of myself forever. I quickly looked away.

When I looked back, she was busy packing up the rest of her lunch tray. Annabelle paused a minute and took out her lip gloss. She put some on, and I smiled as the soft smell of strawberry reached me. She smiled and stood. "We need to get moving, or we'll be late to the next class."

I gathered my stuff and followed the strange redhead.

CHAPTER 17

Solo

Annabelle caught the flu. It was November and I had settled in, in my own way. I went to school with Annabelle. And we sat next to each other. And we ate together. And we came home together. We did homework together, and I would play with Mae or Rico when they wouldn't leave me alone.

Prince watched me. It didn't bother me any because his stare wasn't mean. He was only inspecting my actions. He even joined us when Miss Dixie bought pizza, and we'd watch a movie. We'd all pile on the two couches and laugh until it hurt.

But when Annabelle got sick, my "settled way" was messed up. Walking into math class without her felt strange. I had always looked at others like you would a person in a store. You might see them more than once, but you don't pay much attention. They are nobody to you.

"Where's Annabelle?" A girl with short, blond hair came up next to me. I recognized her. But it took me a minute to remember she sat at the back of the class. She had been nice to me at the beginning of the year. She wore a baggy sweatshirt and was on the chubby side. She wasn't ugly, but not pretty either.

"Sick," I said and turned my head thinking she'd leave me alone.

Instead she sat in Annabelle's seat next to me. "I guess I'll keep you company today. I'm Kelly."

I just stared at her and shook my head. "I don't need a baby-sitter."

Kelly giggled and leaned toward me. "I know that."

I took a deep breath and tried to ignore her the rest of the period.

I thought she'd leave me alone. But I was wrong. I was sitting at the lunch table staring at my chicken leg when a lunch tray plopped down in front of me. I looked up and Kelley was sitting across from me. "I hope you don't mind if we join you."

I didn't have a moment to answer before four others joined the table. Two guys and two girls. One guy, who looked like he could have been my cousin, nodded at me and said, "I'm Dre."

I nodded and looked at the others. The other guy was white with purple hair and the two other girls were twins. They looked Hispanic, but I wasn't sure. Kelly pointed at the girls. "This is Carmen. And this is Carla. They're sisters." The girls giggled. Kelly laughed too. "Well, duh.

That's pretty obvious." Then she pointed at the guys. "You met Dre and that's Tod."

I just nodded at everyone, and then I looked down at my food again. Maybe if I didn't look at them, they would go away.

"So how do you do it?" Tod was leaning in toward me. It was hard to ignore him.

I frowned. "Do what?" They all looked at each other, and I wished I had gotten the flu too.

Dre leaned in too. "Get so close to Annabelle."

I stopped chewing. I sat up straight and looked Dre right in the eye. "What's that supposed to mean?" I felt heat rise.

"Chill!" Dre smiled and returned my look. "It's what you think."

Kelly jumped in. "We've been trying to be friends with her for years. But she pretends we're not even here."

I frowned and put down my chicken leg. "She said no one ever talks to her."

Carmen and Carla spoke over each other, "We've tried, but she doesn't even respond."

I was confused. I looked at Tod and Kelly, and they were just nodding.

"So we wondered, how do you get close to her?" Dre asked again.

I had to think just a minute. The small, strange group wasn't trying to figure me out. They wanted to figure out Annabelle. I wasn't sure how I should respond. Were they going to hurt her? I remembered Rani at the beginning of the year. Were these people as mean as Rani? Then I suddenly got it. I was thinking like Annabelle.

"It's easier to trust no one than someone who might hurt you," I said before I knew I had shared my thoughts out loud. The table was silent. I looked at the group and took a deep breath. "She and I are more alike than I thought."

Dre took a bite of his chicken and looked at me again. "I don't know where the two of you have been, but the whole world isn't out to hurt you."

I shrugged and started eating again.

The next day they left me alone.

CHAPTER 18

Friends

"Why did you tell me no one talks to you?" Annabelle and I were sitting on the bridge. "Because it's true," she stated.

"That's not the story I hear," I said, and watched her start swinging her legs.

She frowned and shook her head. "I'm gone for a few days, and now you know my story better than me?"

"Tell me then." I was serious. "Why do you pretend no one is around? Some kids have been trying to be nice to you."

"You're one to talk. You don't give anyone a chance!" Annabelle was getting angry. She stood up.

I jumped up too and faced her. "We're not talking about me this time. I know I'm an ass. But you're not!" I moved in close and whispered. "Tell me."

She didn't move. Her lips were almost touching mine. But fire was in her eyes as she whispered. "Because I *hate* them. I hate them all!"

"Because you think they're all Rani?" I held my position.

"No." She stayed close in. But I felt a shift. She wanted to be close. She was suddenly afraid. Her voice was so low I had to focus on every word, "Because when I was raped no one cared. I was seven, and after that I couldn't help peeing on myself. Especially when I was upset. But nobody cared. They made fun of me."

My stomach turned. I felt anger build. How could anyone rape a seven-year-old? I wanted to be strong for Annabelle, so I let the anger simmer in my eyes. She saw it. She knew I was angry for her. I held her stare. Then I reached out and wiped the tears that started to fall from her eyes.

We both slowly sat down again. A cool November breeze pushed Annabelle up against me. I put my arm around her. She didn't move away. Something had to change for Annabelle.

The next day we were sitting at lunch. I felt my heart race. I picked up my lunch tray and stood up. She looked at me. I smiled. "Come on!" She sat there a minute before she stood up and followed me.

It wasn't hard to find Kelly's table. Tod's purple hair stood out.

"What are you doing?" Annabelle leaned in close. Her tray almost knocked my tray over.

"You're going to meet some people," I said.

"But ..." Annabelle protested.

I stopped and looked at her. "You were seven. I bet not one of these kids was there." I pointed to Kelly's table. Annabelle looked at them. Really looked at them. "Am I right?" I asked. She just nodded.

We walked up to the table, and I introduced Annabelle to her new friends. It was the strangest thing I'd ever done. It wasn't me. And I sure wasn't going to do it again. But I knew it wasn't about me.

As I sat down I glanced across the lunchroom and saw Prince. For the first time he smiled at me.

CHAPTER 19

Home

I had my first Thanksgiving. I had my first Christmas. They were moments that were different than anything I'd ever felt.

I even started putting up posters on my wall. I had some clothes on each shelf in my closet and books were lined up on my desk.

I turned fifteen that June. Time passed. Seasons passed.

I turned sixteen the following June.

Hugs from Miss Dixie came easily. I even wanted them.

Prince became my friend. He was taking classes at the community college, but still came home every night. He taught me how to use the computer, and we played video games together.

Rico went back to his parents, and we missed his stomping through the house.

Little Mae made me laugh more than once a day. I'd watch her play Barbies, and she'd make up the wildest stories.

Annabelle was growing up. I held her hand a little longer every night at the dinner table, and my insides hurt when she'd walk through the house in her underpants and a T-shirt. Miss Dixie would fuss at her. Then Annabelle would always give me a smile as she'd head up the stairs to put on more clothes.

But I never acted on her smile. I couldn't. We lived in the same house. This was her home. It was my home too.

CHAPTER 20

Clean

This is good news!" Miss Miller was sitting on the couch next to me.

I shook my head. "How is this good news?" I was not sure I could picture my mother drug free. I didn't believe it. Miss Miller couldn't be talking about my mother. She had visited a bunch of times in the last six months. But the times had been awkward. I was always ready for her to leave. I didn't recognize her clean look. I didn't recognize her touch.

The social worker uncrossed her legs. She turned to face me. "TJ, I know it's hard to believe, but she has gone through all the classes and has shown up for her drug tests. She is clean." She paused and then took a deep breath. "And she wants you to come home."

"I can't live with her again. *This* is my home." I had just started my junior year at South High. Two years of school left. I had started to believe this was where I would graduate. At that moment I wished I had never let my guard down. I wished I had stayed in my shell and pushed everyone away. If I had, then the news might have been good.

Miss Dixie came in from the kitchen and put her hand on my shoulder. "TJ, I'm so happy you can call this home. But your mother needs you." She squeezed my shoulder. "Remember, you will always have a place here."

Miss Miller gave Miss Dixie a glare for just a minute and then quickly hid her look with a fake smile. "TJ, you really don't have a choice. The court has granted her full custody of you." I could feel Miss Dixie turn around and stomp off back into the kitchen. She banged a few dishes around before Miss Miller yelled to her, "I know you don't like it, but you're not helping here!"

My chest felt like it was burning. My heart was racing. Trapped. I felt trapped. I didn't have a say. Everything I had come to care about would be gone. Miss Dixie, hot meals, friends, Mae's little hand, and Annabelle.

I looked at Miss Miller and asked, "When?"

She forced another fake smile. "I'll come get you tomorrow at nine."

As she left I sat on the couch and didn't move. I heard footsteps on the stairs. Before I knew it, Mae was jumping in my lap. Big tears started to fall. "First Rico and now you." She put her arms around my neck. "I listened. I couldn't help it." She pointed to the stairs. "But Annabelle started listening." I saw some feet turn and run up the stairs. A few seconds later a door slammed.

I squeezed Mae. "Don't worry. I'm not mad. I would have listened too." She smiled. I took a deep breath so I wouldn't cry. But it was hard. I smiled back. "I guess you'll have to find someone else to pester."

Mae laughed. "I guess so."

CHAPTER 21

Believe in Something

It was late and everyone had gone to bed. I couldn't sleep. There had been no big party, even though Miss Dixie had made my favorite home-made pizza. No one had said much at dinner.

Later I stared out my window at the little bridge. It was lit up by the moon. It looked empty without the redhead dangling her legs. Annabelle hadn't looked at me at dinner. In fact she hadn't said a thing.

The house was so quiet. I was suddenly aware of a noise. It came from above me. I listened so hard that my head started to hurt. I wasn't sure, but it sounded like sobbing. It was Annabelle. I knew then she was crying.

Before I had thought it through, I jumped out of bed and quietly ran up the stairs. I opened her door and quickly closed it behind me. Her room smelled like strawberries.

The crying stopped. "TJ?"

"Yeah, it's me." I stood in the dark and became suddenly aware that I only had on my boxers. My eyes started to adjust. The moonlight came in through her window. I could see Annabelle sitting up in her bed. I whispered, "Are you okay?"

"No." She buried her face in her hands and a small cry escaped.

"Same here." I slowly walked to her bed and sat on the end. "I hate it. I don't know if I can face my old world again." I felt tears roll down my cheeks. I was thankful it was dark. But it didn't matter. She knew. I felt her move in close and touch my face. She wiped away my tears with her fingers.

I took her in my arms and we both cried. Before I knew it, I was lying next to her on the bed. She kissed me. I kissed back. I wanted more.

"I need you, TJ." Annabelle's breath was sweet on my lips.

"I know." I smiled in the dark. "I can't see myself without you."

She was warm. I was hungry. She was willing. I kissed her again. We both wanted more. But I didn't take it.

"What's wrong?" Annabelle spoke so softly. "Don't you want me?"

I touched her cheek and whispered, "For a long time now." I sat up and took the covers and tucked her in. "But not tonight. We can't tonight."

"Why?" She sat up and held my arm.

I put my hand over hers. "Because I don't want it to just be a memory." I reached in and kissed her once more. "I've got to believe it's our future." I smiled. "I've got to believe in something."

Annabelle took my hand and leaned in with her head on my shoulder. "Okay. I'll dream on it too."

CHAPTER 22

Good-bye

Annabelle didn't come down the next morning. I was okay with that. I stood next to Miss Miller's car with a real suitcase in my hand. I had left most of my posters and books. I only took what I knew I would need.

"Here! Take Barbie." Mae held up her favorite Barbie. The blond doll was smiling and wearing her best gold dress. "That way you'll remember me."

I looked at Miss Dixie who nodded for me to take it. I knelt down and gave Mae a hug. "Thank you."

Miss Dixie hugged me and whispered, "I don't care what they say. As far as I'm concerned, you are always welcome here."

I kissed her cheek. "I know."

I was about to get in the car when Prince came up to me. He held out his hand. I took it. He smiled, "TJ, remember. You know who you are."

"Thanks, man!" I smiled and got in the car.

As we pulled out, I looked back at the house I'd called home. Before we turned the corner, I saw a redhead looking out the window at me.

CHAPTER 23

Mom

Clean. That's what she was. Mom was clean. No pot. No meth. No drugs.

But she still had an addiction. And it wasn't me.

"Just give me an hour, baby." Mom spoke softly as she pushed me out the door.

"It's ten, Mom. You really want me on the streets at night?" I shook my head.

Mom yelled to someone behind her, "I'm coming!" She looked at me and smiled. "No, I don't want you on the street. You can sit on the stairs if you want."

We didn't live in the same building where Dad died. We lived in the one next door. The setup was the same. Except my room had a door, and my bed was off the floor.

It only took me two weeks of sitting on the stairs to realize Mom hadn't changed at all. I still didn't matter to her.

"Why did you bring me home?" I asked her as she was pushing me out the door again. Anger was rising.

"Because I love you." She tried to smile. "I miss your dad so much."

I gave her my coldest stare. "Doesn't look like you miss him at all!" It took her one second to slap me. I didn't move. I felt the sting. My cheek felt like it was on fire. But it only pushed the anger inside to the surface.

"Don't you dare talk that way to me, Thomas Jahmal! I loved your father. Why can't I love others too?"

"Whatever!" I turned and left.

I remembered a small card in my back pocket, and I had an idea. I knocked on a neighbor's door. I didn't know the old lady, but she had been watching me for the past two weeks.

"What do you want?" She was peeking at me from behind the chain on her door. Her little white face looked so pale I was afraid she was going to have a heart attack.

"Excuse me, ma'am. I was wondering if I could use your phone." She stared. "I need to call social services and report my mother." I waved the small business card I had gotten from Miss Miller before she left.

I could tell the lady was thinking. I waited. She finally said, "Okay, but wait there!" A few moments later she handed me a cell phone through the crack in the door. She continued to stare at me as I dialed.

"Hello?" Miss Miller's voice sounded like I woke her up.

"Listen!" I said. "This is TJ and this is not working. You need to take me back to Miss Dixie."

Miss Miller put on her best counseling voice. "Now TJ, let's talk about this. What's going on?"

I told her. I told her how I spent my evenings in the stairwell. Finally I sighed, "So will you come and get me?"

The voice on the other side spoke slowly. "It's not that easy. I will call the police, and we'll do a home visit."

"When?"

"Tomorrow." Before she said anything else, I hung up and cussed.

I handed the wide-eyed lady the phone. "Thanks," I said and turned. I heard the door close behind me.

CHAPTER 24

The Visit

I was sixteen.

There was food in the fridge. I could feed myself.

I had clothes. I could wash my clothes.

I could get myself to school.

There was no sign of neglect.

Mom promised that she wouldn't make me sit outside anymore.

Miss Miller and the police found there was no need for concern. I needed to give my mother a chance.

I never called Miss Miller again.

CHAPTER 25

Back

Mom kept her promise. I found myself alone at home most evenings, which was better than sitting on the stairs. Sometimes she'd bring someone home. She didn't say anything to me, but I would grab my jacket and leave. But I wouldn't sit on the stairs. I had to get out.

It was getting cooler. I had been home a month. I felt like I was trying to figure out who I was all over again. I made sure I didn't stand out at North High. I went to classes and came home. Most kids recognized me but stayed clear. They remembered the old me. I told myself that was a good thing.

I missed everyone in that house that sat across from Grant Park. I didn't have a phone so I couldn't call. Mom was always out of minutes on her phone and told me she'd get me a phone as soon as she got some money. I tried not to think of Annabelle. It hurt too bad. But I couldn't help it. I hadn't smiled or laughed since I'd left.

I headed to the gas station a block away. I knew they would be open this late. I had a couple of dollars in my pocket and thought I might as well get a Coke.

"Hey, TJ." Kaden's voice hadn't changed. He was leaning against the wall as I came out the door.

I looked at him and nodded. "Hey. What's up?" I acted like no time had passed.

He looked at me with a smile that made my stomach turn. "I heard you were back. Why didn't you come by?"

I opened my Coke and took a sip. "No reason really. Not gotten around to it yet. Been busy."

"Liar." Kaden stared at me.

I started to walk away. But he came right up next to me. He tried to sound like a friend, but his voice sounded pissed. "Look man, sorry about your dad. But come on, you disappear for two years. When you get back you don't talk to your friends. Why is that?"

I stopped and turned to face Kaden. I'd grown and was as tall as he was. He looked skinnier than I remembered, and his teeth showed signs of decay. "So it looks like gang life has been good to you."

He grinned. "So you know we're a gang. Good. I think you need to come on back to us and make it official." He grabbed my Coke and took a sip. Then he handed it back. "You know we look out for each other."

I stared at him. I didn't look away. I wanted to throw the can on the street. But I took a sip. It was so cold. I wished I had bought a coffee instead. I felt my teeth start to chatter. "Don't think so. I'll stay in my own world until I can get out of here." Then I started walking again.

Kaden didn't run after me. Instead his voice boomed, "You owe us, TJ." I didn't look back. But I knew this wasn't the end of Kaden Cruz.

I could still hear my Dad's voice. "It's not free. You'll have to pay them back one day."

CHAPTER 26

Beat Down

Staying off the streets at night didn't help. One afternoon I'd jumped off the school bus. I didn't think to look at anything around me. I should have noticed the mothers quickly grabbing their children. But I didn't. The sound of the bus pulling away hid the sound of the feet running up behind me.

I felt my book bag jerked off my shoulder. One person punched my face while someone else kicked me. It took me a minute before I started swinging. At anything. I heard someone yell. But a harder punch followed. I finally was able to make out a white arm and a black arm. My eyes were covered with something dark, making it too hard to see the faces.

I heard screaming. "Stop it! I'll call the police!"

Still the kicks and punches came. One hard kick to my stomach made me finally stop fighting back. I curled up in a ball and waited. But the throbbing in my head was too much. Everything went dark.

CHAPTER 27

Billy

I wasn't out long. I felt arms grabbing me and pulling me up. I could make out a familiar face. One I hadn't seen in years. Billy was bigger than me. He towered over me and picked me up like I weighed nothing. I felt myself laughing at myself. How did I ever bully this guy? I could still see him holding his mother's hand at the bus stop.

"You've grown," was all I could whisper.

"Shut up, man!" Billy carried me carefully to my apartment building. "You got a good beating." I could barely hear him whisper, "I'm sure you deserved it."

"Billy!" I could hear a woman's voice. It must have been his mother. "No one deserves a beating."

I heard Billy grunt, "Whatever." He shifted my weight and I groaned. I suddenly puked. I heard Billy cuss, but he didn't drop me.

"Sorry," I said, knowing it wouldn't help.

Once we reached my door, I heard my mother cry as they carried me into my room. She was running around getting wet towels to clean me up. Billy's mom helped.

Billy stood in my room and stared at me for a minute. I didn't care. Then his eyes looked at something sitting on my window sill. "Nice Barbie!" He was laughing. I didn't care.

I turned to look at the plastic doll. She was still wearing her golden dress and was smiling at me. "She reminds me of where I want to be."

"Dressed like a girl?" Billy was teasing.

He made me smile. "Yeah, right!" I joked back. "No, a special little girl gave it to me and it reminds me that one day I will get out of here."

There was a long pause. Billy turned to go, and then he looked back at me. "You've changed."

I smiled at him. "I hope so."

CHAPTER 28

Truth

Mom cleaned me up and slept on the floor next to me that night. I could hear her crying off and on. I had never known my mother to cry over me. But there was something about it that helped me sleep.

The next morning Mom brought me a bowl of cornflakes and some juice while I was still in bed. I looked at her funny. She was dressed, and she had pulled her hair back into a tight bun. But her eyes were puffy.

"Thanks." I took the juice. My lip stung like crazy as I tried to take a sip. My whole face felt like it was swollen. I didn't want to look in the mirror. Not yet.

"I think you should stay home from school today." Mom stated the obvious. "I already called the school and told them what happened."

I just nodded as I awkwardly spooned cornflakes into my mouth.

"I should have let you stay where you were," Mom suddenly said. I stopped eating and looked up at her with confusion. She reached for Barbie and held her like a priceless object. "I should have let you stay."

"What do you mean?" I was starting to see my mother for the first time. She was trying to talk to me. She was trying to tell me something. Something that wasn't filled with lies.

She looked me in the eyes. "I'm so sorry." She looked back down at the doll and played with her dress. "But I needed the money. I needed the money that I get from the state to help support a child." She looked back at me.

I felt anger rise. I put my bowl down on the floor and leaned back in my bed. I stared at the ceiling trying to calm myself.

Mom continued, "I don't want you to end up like your father." I didn't say anything. "It started the same way."

I looked at her again. "What started?"

She placed Barbie back on the window sill and tried to touch my leg. I pulled away. She dropped her eyes. "He said no and was beat up." I listened. "He pushed them away so many times until he couldn't take living in fear. So he bought drugs from them. Instead of joining them. This kept them off his back."

"What are you saying?"

"He always thought he was a failure because he could never join the gang. He never wanted to. He was too afraid." Tears started to fall. "So he lived as far away from the real world as he could. High."

I could feel so much anger well up. But I could also feel fear overshadow everything.

"Well, I am not my father!" I lied.

Mom just looked at me. She nodded and stood up. She knew I was just like my father.

CHAPTER 29

Not My Father

I refused to be my father. The next morning I got dressed and went for a walk. I had to clear my head. I would not let the gang force me into using their drugs. But what could I do? If I joined the Vipers they'd make me hurt others, but if I didn't, I'd live in fear of more beatings.

I couldn't really leave the neighborhood. Mom and Dad had broken off family ties a long time ago. I pushed away thoughts of Miss Dixie's. I would be made to return home if I tried to go there. I had nowhere to go.

Something had to change. I had to call my own shots. Suddenly I knew I would have a better chance to live without fear if I was on the inside of the gang. This way I would have a chance to survive.

CHAPTER 30

The Hillside Vipers

The knock on the door of the yellow house came easy to me. I had to knock five times before anyone heard it. The TV was blasting.

The door opened. Brian's surprised look made that moment worth it. His left eye was still purple. I knew then he gave me my blue and purple marks on my face. "What do you want?" He tried to sound tough.

"I need to talk to BB." I pushed my fear away. I held the image of my father in my head and let my anger control my mood.

Brian opened the door wider. He stepped to the side and yelled, "BB!"

I could see Snake and Bulldog walking around inside, and Candy was flirting with Kaden. BB made his way around the small crowd and walked up to the door. He was bigger than a couple of years ago. He looked like he had aged more than just two years. He must have been twenty-two but fat was beginning to form under his chin, making him look almost thirty.

His arms still looked like two bowling balls every time he flexed. He liked to flex. It was working. His sheer strength made me second guess why I was standing in front of him. He looked me up and down and smiled. "So you must be TJ. I recognized you from your messed up face." A roar of laughter spilled from behind him. BB was blocking my view, but I heard

Kaden's voice. I just stood there and put on the best tough look I could pull off.

BB's eyes narrowed, "What do you want?"

"I'm ready." I stuck out my chin and held steady.

"For what?" BB kept staring.

My eyes didn't move. "You already gave me a beating in. Doesn't that mean I'm in the gang?"

BB suddenly laughed. He repeated to the guys what I had said, and then they were all laughing. In fact, BB was laughing so hard his eyes started watering. I just stood there with my heart racing. After a few minutes he grabbed my shoulder and pulled me into the yellow house. "Come in! I haven't laughed so hard in a long time." He shoved me down on the couch next to Kaden. A bruise on Kaden's hand confirmed his role in my beating. But it didn't seem to bother Kaden. He was smiling too. Candy was sitting on the other side of him with her arm around his neck.

"See, I knew you'd come around." Kaden spoke like we were long-lost friends. I just smiled and pushed down my need to puke.

Brian handed me a Coke. "If I remember right," he said. I nodded, opened it, and took a sip. It felt good.

"So you want to be part of the Hillside Vipers?" BB took a sip of beer as he settled back on the other couch. The TV was still blasting.

"Yeah!" I took another sip. A few more guys walked out of the back room to see what was going on.

"Why?" BB held his beer on his knee.

I started to shift my body but stopped. I didn't want to look uneasy. "Because Kaden said you look out for each other. I'm tired of looking out for myself." I hadn't actually lied. It was half way true. I *was* tired of looking out for myself. BB saw the truth in my eyes.

The big man nodded at Brian to turn off the TV. The only white boy in the room moved quickly and silence filled the room. "Okay, TJ. You have to earn your way in." BB smiled. "This doesn't involve pissing on any packages either." Everyone laughed. I forced myself to join in, even though that memory reminded me how weak I really was.

I nodded and finished off my Coke. "What is it?"

"You've got to beat down someone." BB's voice was serious.

"Who?" I asked as if it were no big deal.

"Someone who shouldn't be on our turf," BB spoke clearly.

"Where do I find him?" I asked.

"Or her?" Candy laughed.

I felt my stomach turn, but I held my eyes steady. BB looked at Candy and told her to shut up. Then he looked back at me. "The Church Street Pit Bulls like to come through our turf. They try to take a short cut to the bowling alley. Watch for the sign of a Pit Bull and take one down."

I paused a minute, feeling stupid. But I had to ask. "What sign?"

The guys laughed a minute before BB answered, "They wear these stupid dog collars." I nodded remembering seeing some guys with dog collars hanging outside my elementary school on Church Street.

"When?" I asked knowing the answer.

BB smiled. "We got nothing better to do." He stood up and headed for the door. "Let's go hang out at the bowling alley. The rest of the guys in the room nodded, but Candy protested a little. Kaden kissed her, and she smiled and joined the guys as they walked out the door.

I put down my empty can and followed the Hillside Vipers. The cool breeze felt good on my bruised face. My whole body still hurt. I wished I had at least waited a few more days before I had the bright idea to join a gang.

CHAPTER 31

Initiation

The rest of the gang went inside the bowling alley with BB. They had me wait outside next to the flashing beer sign. The cool air was starting to feel cold. I jumped around a little trying to keep warm. The idea was for them to look for someone inside while I stood watch outside. It was an hour before they came out laughing. BB looked at me. They all laughed again, this time at me. "Better luck next time." I followed the group back to the yellow house half frozen to death.

The next night was the same. And the next. I was starting to get pissed. They were making a fool of me. And I was letting them.

The third night I wore as many clothes as I could fit under my jacket. I even had on my mother's purple hat. The guys laughed at me all the way to the bowling alley. I didn't care. They were inside having a good time. At least I was warm.

"Did your mother dress you?" A strange voice made me turn and look at two guys walking up to me. One was white and the other black. Trying to look tough in the cold, they only had on T-shirts and jeans. I could clearly see the dog collars they wore around their necks.

Suddenly I punched the guy who spoke to me in the mouth. I was thankful that I had had a few extra days to recover from my own beating. The punch took the guy by surprise. He crashed to the ground. The white guy, slightly shorter than me, cussed at me and took a swing at my stomach. All the extra clothing softened his blow. I took my knee to his groin. He tumbled over.

I heard someone yell, "Fight!" from inside the building. Soon people came out to watch. By then I had pounced on the first guy and hit him in the face until I saw blood dripping from his nose. The second guy came up on me from behind. He grabbed my head but only managed to pull off my mother's hat while I took a swing at his stomach. He cussed again and fell down.

"Get out of here now!" I heard Kaden's voice as I saw him running off behind the bowling alley. I was confused at first. But that's when I heard the sirens. Someone had called the police. I took off running too.

By the time I reached the yellow house, I was sweating. I stripped off all the clothes as the rest of the gang sat on the couches staring at me. I looked at them and asked, "What?"

They all started laughing. Brian finally said, "I never knew having on so many clothes could actually help you in a fight." I looked at the pile of clothes I had shed. I felt like a sumo wrestler that had just dropped two hundred pounds. I started laughing. We all laughed.

I didn't go home that night.

CHAPTER 32

Chains

I didn't get my chain tattoo right away. I still had to earn it. A piece at a time. I learned that each link of the chain was tattooed on its own. Like a Boy Scout earns his badge. I got two small circles tattooed on a part of my wrist. One circle for each guy I beat down. I looked at BB's chain and noticed it wrapped around his wrist several times like a snake starting to crawl up his arm.

"Cool, huh?" Kaden caught me running my finger across the small circles. I didn't look at him. I just nodded. I realized

I would have to fill the chain up with more links. I would always look weak until I hurt enough people to complete my chain. Even then I would have to grow my chain to be respected like BB.

Fear welled up. I pushed it away. Anger welled up. I embraced it. I would need all the anger I could hold on to—to survive.

I went home that night. I took Mae's gift out of my window. I walked into the kitchen and lifted the lid of the trash can. The blond doll was smiling at me. I threw her in the trash. For a moment I looked at the doll with her hair covered in coffee grounds. Then I closed the lid and turned to walk away.

"What are you doing?" Mom stood in the doorway.

I looked at her and spoke slowly. "That's not my world anymore."

"TJ, what are you up to?" Mom was worried. This new mother came too late.

"The school called, and you haven't been there in days."

I stared at Mom and just shrugged. "I've got better things to do."

I turned to go, and she grabbed my arm. Before I could move away, she saw the two small circles. A quiet cuss word fell from her lips. She looked at me. She looked pale. She dropped my arm. "I guess you do." She turned and walked back into the living room.

CHAPTER 33

High

I had planned on never being high. Not like my mom. Not like my dad. But I wasn't sure how I would pull this off. I watched the guys in the gang. They got bored. They got high. Or drunk. Or both.

Sex was a way to fill the time too. Candy seemed willing when anyone was ready. The other girls preferred to stick with one person. BB had Val. It was short for her last name, Valdez. She was about BB's age. Long dark hair, a beautiful body, and a slight Hispanic accent made her stand out. I guessed BB took the best. But she made it clear she wasn't always for the taking. Her chain tattoo wrapped around her wrist twice.

"What's your problem?" Candy asked me as I felt her hand rest on my knee. I wanted to push the hand away. I didn't. I knew that would make me look like I wasn't playing the same game.

"What are you talking about?" I looked at her.

"I'm not dumb." She spoke so others could hear. Kaden was walking back from the kitchen with a beer in his hand. Candy continued, "You never get high. You never get so messed up you can't see straight." Then she whispered in my ear, "And you never want me."

By now Kaden was not happy with Candy whispering in my ear. He shoved her over and sat between us. He had heard most of what she'd said. He looked at me and frowned. "Yeah! What's up with that?"

I shrugged and said, "Not my thing." I stood up to head into the kitchen. BB was standing in the doorway. I walked past him.

"Wait a minute." BB's voice stopped me. "Candy's right." I turned to look at him. But my eyes were steady. I had mastered hiding any fear. "You never get high."

I didn't miss a beat. "Neither do you." I had him. I had been watching him. Sometimes he drank and smoked a little. But he was never out of control.

BB didn't catch the difference between doing a little drugs versus no drugs at all. He only saw the reality of the situation. He was never high either. For a minute I saw his eyes waver. He knew I knew his secret. This was how he kept control of the gang. I dropped my eyes. I did not want him to think I was challenging him.

"Sure he gets high!" Brian came over half drunk and slapped BB on the back. "We've partied together tons!"

BB shoved Brian down on the couch. He walked over to me. He got really close. "I don't know what your game is, boy!"

"No game." I looked at him again. "Just want a clear head like you. Want to be ready when you need me." It was easy to lie now. It didn't even feel like I was lying.

BB's eyes changed. He smiled. He pulled me into a back room. I had never been there before. I knew it had to be where he slept. A mattress was on the floor, and he had his own TV. There was a table with all sorts of papers and bags. He reached into one bag and handed me a phone. "Here! I think you're ready."

I ran my fingers along the cell phone. I flipped up its top and flipped it back down again. "What's this for?"

"It's for you. You can make calls and I will pay the bill. But you can also be reached by me anytime I need you to make a drop." BB was talking to me like we were friends. He looked at me again. "You're right. Sometimes I need someone who isn't high."

I felt my body relax. It worked. I wouldn't have to dive into the drug addiction that took my father's life. But when BB walked out the door reality hit. I would have to sell the drugs to those who were just like my father. Did that make me better than him? Or worse? I couldn't tell anymore.

CHAPTER 34

Call

I went home that night. I needed some time to myself. Mom left me alone. She didn't have a boyfriend over that night. I held the new phone in my hand and my heart raced. I pulled out Miss Dixie's number and stared at it. I couldn't let my other life go. I decided to call and hoped Annabelle would answer.

As the phone rang my chest filled with such pain. I could still hear Annabelle's voice in my head. I still felt Mae's hug. I could still hear Prince telling me *remember who you are*. I didn't know anymore. I suddenly thought if Annabelle answered I would have to lie. I would have to tell her I was doing great. And I wasn't.

"Hello?" It was Annabelle. I couldn't breathe. "Hello?" Annabelle spoke again. I could almost smell her strawberry lip gloss. "Hello? Is anybody there?"

I wanted to answer. But I couldn't. I hung up and cried.

I finally pulled myself together and called on my anger to replace my tears.

CHAPTER 35

Drop

I was right. One afternoon in the middle of a party BB pulled me into his room. "I need you to make this drop." He handed me a package that was flat. He showed me how to shove it into the upper part of my pants and pull my shirt down over the rest of it.

"What do I do?" I asked like we were talking about how to play my first card game.

BB didn't smile. His eyes showed just a little worry. I knew this was no prank. This was the real thing. "Walk around the corner to Park Street. Go a block until you get to

Jackson Park. Keep walking around. Don't stop and look around. A car will pull up next to you, and they will have their music turned off. Stop and lean in like you are being asked directions. Point down the street and give directions. Then get in the car. Make the exchange in the car, and they will drop you off at the corner of the next street."

I nodded. "How will they know it's me?"

BB walked to the one small closet he had. He opened it. It was full of different team jackets. "Today's drop will be a Chicago Bear's drop." He handed me a navy jacket with orange cuffs and collar. An orange C stood out clearly on the back.

"Cool," I said feeling suddenly childlike. I had never worn a team's jacket before.

BB smiled for just a minute. Then he told me I needed to go. The drop was happening in twenty minutes. He led me to a back door. I had never gone out this way. But he knew walking through the party would draw too much attention. "Come back this way too."

I nodded. As I walked away from the yellow house, I felt my stomach turn. A few flurries started to fall. I shivered. I was thankful for the warmth of the jacket. I walked as normally as I could with a package shoved down my pants.

It only took me ten minutes to get to Jackson Park. As I got closer, I tried to slow down some. It wasn't really a park anymore. It was mostly concrete with six basketball hoops marking the edges of the park. A handful of guys had a game going. I wondered how long their game would last since the snowflakes were getting larger. A few cuss words told me they were almost done.

They didn't pay any attention to me. Neither did the old lady walking her dog or the young couple trying to carry their grocery bags inside.

A car pulled up next to me. I forced myself not to turn and look. I could hear music blasting. The car kept going. A second car was behind the first. Its music blasted too. But then the music died. It was the right car.

I noticed the old lady suddenly turn her head to look at me as I turned to face the car. She quickly pulled her dog into the old house directly behind her. So much for going unnoticed.

I leaned into the window and was facing a man who looked like he could be my father. I was surprised. I expected a teenager with nothing better to do. Not a man, who was most likely a father.

"What?" The man's voice broke my look. "You got a problem?"

"No problem." I pulled myself together. I pointed down the road like I was giving directions. Then I got into the backseat of the car.

Few words were spoken.

The smell of cigarettes and sour clothes made me want to roll down the window so I could breathe. But I didn't. I saw a package on the seat next to me. "Is this for me?" I asked like a young child asking for candy.

The man cussed. "Did BB send an idiot?"

I felt my blood rise. "Just want to do it right my first time. I'm the best BB has at four in the afternoon."

The man started laughing. "So you're BB's new boy!"

I didn't mean to sound angry, but I couldn't help it. "I'm nobody's boy!"

The car stopped and the man looked back at me. "We'll see. Now leave me my stuff and get out." I pulled the package out of my pants and shoved the new one into its place. I didn't say anything else. I got out, slammed the door, and started walking back to the yellow house.

I didn't notice how cold I was as the snow fell harder. My shoes were wet. I was too angry to care.

I ran in the back door and opened BB's door without knocking. Big mistake. BB and Val were making out. I was lucky to get out with just a cussing. He told me to wait outside the door.

So I sat down at the foot of the paper-thin door. I could hear noises that caused my insides to ache for Annabelle. I pushed the thought away and let anger take its place.

I had a wad of money stuck down the back of my pants.

I was sitting and waiting.

My shoes were wet.

Maybe I was BB's boy.

I tried to tell myself that was better than BB's enemy.

CHAPTER 36

Strange Request

I need you to go back to school." BB woke me up early one January morning. Christmas had passed without much attention. BB threw one big party. But that wasn't much different than other days.

"What?" I sat up on the couch that had become my regular sleeping spot. "What are you talking about?" I had gotten used to making drops. Sometimes, though, I was confused when he only had me do drops where he was sure it would go smoothly. He sent Brian or Kaden to the more risky locations. I figured he was still training me.

"I need you to go back to school," BB repeated. I had become comfortable with drop offs and switching between the different team jackets. I had proven myself in a handful of fights. This request from BB took me by surprise.

"What are you, my mother now?" I asked him. "I missed all last semester. I don't know if they'll take me back."

"You were a good student, right?" BB asked.

I frowned, totally confused. "I guess so. I made it through ninth and tenth grade without much problem. But that was ..." I caught myself before I started talking about South High.

"Good. Get up and get out the door." BB smiled. "I need a person on the inside of the school again. It's been awhile since I've had anyone on the inside to sell for me."

My stomach turned. "You want me to pretend to want to go back to school, so I can find new customers?"

BB slapped me on the back. "See how smart you are. You should be in school."

"Very funny," I said as I put on a clean shirt. I drank some OJ right from the bottle and grabbed my jacket. Before I left, I looked back at BB. It was just the two of us. Everyone else was passed out upstairs. I sighed and then spoke, "You realize for me to stay in school and make this believable I actually have to do the work. I might even have homework."

BB grinned. "See! You are already the perfect one for being inside. It will come naturally to you."

Suddenly BB had that same look again. The one he gave me when I did my first drop. I couldn't tell if it was worry or what. But he hid it quickly by cussing at me to get on out the door. I might be late.

I shook my head the whole way around the corner and down the block.

I wasn't sure if I should be excited to get back into school or if I should be angry at BB for jerking me around like his puppet.

CHAPTER 37

Between Bells

It felt strange sitting in the classroom again. I had managed to get into the Algebra 2 class. That was a shock for many of my fellow classmates. The school had welcomed me as a returning student. They seemed ready to save me all over again.

"What are you doing here?" Billy sat in the desk next to me.

I looked at the big boy who had carried my broken body home. I looked at the boy who knew the secret of my golden Barbie. I looked at him and lied, "I'm here to learn." I smiled and continued, "You even told me I'd changed."

Billy shook his head, "Yeah. That was before ..." He stopped.

"Before what?" I asked like I was confused.

Billy leaned over and whispered. "TJ, you're not fooling anyone. We know you belong to the Hillside Vipers." He rolled his eyes. "We're not blind." His eyes rested on the small incomplete chain that was beginning to wrap around my wrist.

I touched it, quickly realizing how stupid I was to forget that the tattoo would give me away. After a moment I said, "Well I was, but it wasn't for me."

Billy leaned back in his chair. "Whatever!" He looked at me and said, "It's not easy to get out. It's not like you just decide one day to change your hairstyle." Then he leaned in again. "Look, TJ. It's your business. Just leave me out of it, okay?"

I could see Billy wasn't being tough. He was being brave. He was asking for a favor and I owed him. I nodded and said, "Okay." Billy turned around and looked at the teacher who had just walked in the door.

I turned and paid attention to her too. My heart raced just a little as she handed me the textbook. I ran my hand across the cover. I opened the book and listened to the teacher. My mind started gathering new information. It felt strange to think about something else other than what BB would ask me to do next. Those moments lasted no longer than an hour at a time. When the last bell rang, I felt myself search for the tough TJ that had to live out on the streets.

I found myself getting to school on time and diving into my work. The rest of the gang teased me, but BB would cuss them, and they'd leave me alone.

It only took a week before kids found me. The kids who would be customers. They looked for my chain. I realized that

BB hadn't sent me earlier because my chain wasn't long enough yet. Once others found me, it was easy. We agreed on a time, and then the drop off took place off campus. This way the school drug dogs left me alone, and I could keep pretending I was a regular student. At least between bells.

CHAPTER 38

Church Street
Pit Bulls

I wasn't alone. I don't know if I just didn't want to see it. Maybe I thought the Hillside Vipers ruled North Side High. I was wrong.

It was quite simple. I had customers. So I had enemies. The Church Street Pit Bulls started making themselves known. They weren't happy.

I was sitting at a lunch table and actually studying. Someone sat down across from me. I thought it might be someone who wanted to do business. When I looked up I saw a huge boy. He was so big and black.

I'd never noticed him before. His eyes narrowed just as I noticed his dog collar. "Get out or the Hillside Vipers will pay."

"But I go to school here." I tried to sound tough, but it came out weak.

"You know what I mean." He stood up and stepped behind me. Before I could move, he had me pinned down on the table. I could hardly breathe. His fish breath whispered, "Only room for one seller in this school!" I felt my face get warm. I couldn't speak. I could hear people starting to yell. He leaned in one more time. "Tell BB I could have killed you. If you don't stop selling, then next time I won't be so nice!" He squeezed me one last time. Suddenly he was gone.

I felt myself pass out.

I must have been out for a few minutes. When I came to I was still slumped over my table with my head on my book. "You okay?" Billy's familiar voice made me turn my head. He was standing near me with a small crowd gathered around him. He didn't touch me. He just looked at me with a told-you-so look.

"Yeah. I'm fine," I whispered. My voice was scratchy.

I sat up and watched Billy lead the crowd away.

"Mr. Young?" A man's voice I recognized as one of the intake counselors was behind me. Mr. Beck had helped me get back into school. He just came up to me like he hadn't seen a thing that had happened. So I sat up as straight as I could and pretended I was okay.

"Yes, Mr. Beck?" His pale skin gave away the dark circles under his eyes. But he tried to smile. "You have a visitor."

"What?" I asked. I stood up and packed my books into my bag. I followed Mr. Beck out of the cafeteria. I had no idea who would be visiting me at school.

CHAPTER 39

Visitor

The office area was stuffy and smelled like gym socks. Mr. Beck walked me past the front desk and into his office. The room was small and two chairs faced a small metal desk. One of the chairs was taken. It only took me a second to recognize those legs.

Miss Miller turned to smile at me. She got up and greeted me, "TJ, I'm so glad to see you again." She wanted to hug me, but settled for an awkward handshake. She nodded at Mr. Beck who turned to leave. He closed the door behind him.

"Miss Miller? What are you doing here?" I looked at her like she was crazy.

"Come sit with me a minute, TJ." She pointed at the chair next to hers. We both sat. I waited for her to explain herself. "I've been looking for you. I've tried to check up on you a couple of times, but your Mom always said you were out."

At first I smiled at my mother's willingness to cover for me. But then I realized she was probably ashamed. "I was out," I said. I shifted in my seat. "I've been busy."

Miss Miller watched me pull my sleeve down, so she couldn't see my tattoo. She shook her head just a little. "TJ, you haven't been in school."

"I am now." I was defensive. Miss Miller's preachy style was bothering me again. I sucked air through my teeth. "You're not my mother." I stood up and started to walk to the door. I had my hand on the door and paused. I looked at her and said, "I don't know what you want. You pop in and out of my life pretending you care or can help. But I can see right through you. You're so full of it. You have never helped me." I turned to go.

"TJ!" Miss Miller was standing too. She had fire in her eyes. But not mean. She was hurt. "How dare you!" She started pointing her finger at me. "I have helped you as best I could."

"Yeah, right! You took me away from this hell hole. You put me in a place where I believed I could start another life. Then you brought me back here. When I called on you to help ..." I paused trying to push away the tears. I kept them under control. "You left me hanging." Tears were flowing down Miss Miller's cheeks. I whispered, "So I'm on my own. I'm trying to survive!"

I turned to go again. This time I felt her hand on my shoulder. "Please, TJ, sit down and hear me out." She said it honestly. So I moved back to my chair and listened. "You're right. I should have fought for you to stay with Miss Dixie. But that's not how the system works. We have to place children back with their parents. I did try to check on you, but you were already gone before I had a chance." She lowered her eyes. "Not that I could have helped much." She looked back at me. "You see, there isn't much money. The program to follow up with foster kids and offer support is struggling."

"Duh!" I sucked air through my teeth again.

"Let me finish," she said gently. "I came here to tell you something. You need to hear me on this." She tried to look me straight in the eye. I let her. "I can't save you. You have to do that on your own."

I started to laugh. "Oh, this is really big news. Isn't that what I'm doing?"

Miss Miller leaned back in the chair and smiled. "Is it?" We sat there in silence for a few minutes. "You may not know this, but you do have choices you can make. You can choose, TJ." She whispered again, "You can choose."

Choice was a hard concept for me. I always felt I had to do what made the most sense at the time. Even if it went against my gut reaction. I did it. I had to. I was confused, "But I can't really choose. Miss Miller, I have to do what I have to do. I have no choice."

This time she stood. She reached out and put her hand on my shoulder. "TJ, you never trusted me. I'm sorry about that. But trust me now. Choose your future." She bent down and looked me straight in the eye. "And I promise you, I won't get in your way."

She stood again and left.

I wasn't sure what she meant by that last line. My head was racing. On one hand she tells me I have a choice. On the other hand I have the Church Street Pit Bulls threatening my life. I didn't see how I had any choice but to defend myself.

CHAPTER 40

Pit Bull Down

I didn't tell BB about Miss Miller's visit. There were more important things to talk about. I wanted to know what to do about the threat from the Pit Bulls. Should I keep going to school?

"Sure you should keep going." BB looked at me like the whole thing was as simple as learning to share toys on a playground. "The Church Street Pit Bulls are more bark than bite."

"I could sure feel his bite in the lunch room," I protested. "I don't think he was messing around."

BB looked at me like I was declaring defeat. "Are you giving up? Are you afraid?" His voice was rising. "Around here, I determine what we do next. We never give in to the Pit Bulls. This is our turf. They're the ones who need to back off." I shut up and watched him pace. He stopped and opened the door and yelled, "Brian, Kaden, get in here!" Before I knew it, BB had given the two guys directions. They needed to find the Pit Bull who threatened me before school started. Then they were to beat him down.

Once Brian and Kaden left, I looked at BB "Why didn't you ask me to beat him down?"

"'Cause I need you in school. I can't have you expelled." BB shook his head. "TJ, you have to be my inside man. Now get out of here."

Brian and Kaden had no problem finding the big Church Street Pit Bull. They beat him bad. Right in front of the school. Kaden used a brick. He slammed it into the big guy's head as other kids screamed for them to stop. I wanted to scream too. It took longer than they thought to beat him down, so by the time the guy stopped moving, the police had arrived.

I stood back as I watched Kaden and Brian try to run. They didn't get far. The cops cuffed them. I watched as Kaden and Brian were hauled off in the back of a police car. Meanwhile, I heard the siren of an ambulance. The flashing lights came around the corner warning people to get out of the way. Within minutes, two men dressed in blue jumped out of the back of the ambulance. They ran over to pick up what was left of the big, bloody mass lying on the sidewalk.

I felt my stomach turn. I closed my
eyes for one minute to pull myself together. I turned to walk into the school with the
rest of the students. I caught a glimpse of
Billy. He looked at me. I just looked away.

CHAPTER 41

Drive-By

I didn't take my usual way back to the house that afternoon. Even an idiot knew the Church Street Pit Bulls would be pissed. I didn't want to be an easy target. Weaving my way through some back streets did help some. I walked up the back steps of the yellow house later than normal. This meant I wasn't sitting in my usual place, on my favorite couch, in the living room at that moment. It meant I wasn't facing the front of the house. It meant I didn't get hit in the chest with bullets as the Church Street Pit Bulls unloaded their guns on the yellow house. The house I had started to call my home.

I flattened myself on the top step as I heard the first round of bullets fly. Screams and curses filled my head with fear. I pushed open the back door and slid my body inside. I could see down the hall into the living room. Snake and Candy were lying on the floor. Blood slowly oozed around their heads. I stood up. Val and BB came running from the back room. BB's eyes were on fire. I could see the automatic gun in the big man's hand. Val screamed as he shoved her back into the room.

I could hear tires burning in the street. They were turning around. BB saw me and cussed. "Get down. And stay there!" I forced myself down and kept my face pressed to the hard wood floor.

"What are you doing?" I yelled at BB, who was obviously not staying down.

"I'm going to give them something to come back for." He grabbed the gun with both hands and ran into the living room.

As I heard him hit the floor, the second round of bullets went flying. This time they were coming from the living room. I could hear the car race away.

Suddenly, there was silence. I didn't stand up. Not yet. Sweat dripped off my nose as I crawled into the front room. BB was sitting on the floor. The gun was lying at his side. I slowly stood up, looking out the window. Then I looked at BB again. He reached out a hand to me, and I took it to pull him up. Or at least try to. As he stood with his back to the window, he looked at the two bodies lying on the floor and sighed. Then he patted my face. Something he'd never done. "At least you're not hurt. And Kaden and Brian are at the police station. They'll be back."

What BB and I didn't realize was that there were two Pit Bull cars. The second one drove up so quietly. They had a perfect shot of BB's back. They took it. The sound of bullets flew once more. BB's eyes opened wide in surprise. He crashed forward onto me and took me down to the floor. My fear kept me from realizing what had just happened. I let the massive dead body cover me as I waited for the silence to return. It was several minutes before my heart caught up with my mind. I didn't even try not to cry. BB was dead. Snake was dead. Candy was dead. I struggled to get BB off of me.

Suddenly, a scream came from behind me. Val had left the bedroom and was soon pounding on BB's body. She was yelling at someone who would never hear her again. "I told you not to come out here! I *told you*!"

I realized the police would show up soon. I looked at the makeup-smeared Val and yelled, "Val, help me get BB off of me." She whimpered as we both shoved him to the side. My jacket was soaked in BB's blood. As I stood, she continued to kneel over her man. I touched her shoulder. "We've got to go! The police are coming."

I ran into the back bedroom and grabbed the Chicago Bears jacket. I knew Val would need one too, so I grabbed a blue Boston Red Sox jacket with a single red *B* on the front. I took off my blood-soaked jacket and T-shirt and threw the Chicago Bears jacket on. I started to run back out of the room, but I stopped in front of the table. I realized the police would take everything. I reached into one of the brown bags still sitting on the table ready for business. I grabbed two handfuls of cash and shoved the money in the pockets of my jacket and the Red Sox Jacket. I didn't stop to count.

I could hear sirens. I ran back into the living room and grabbed Val. She threw on her jacket. She wiped snot from her nose and let me take her by the hand as we ran out the back door.

We just ran.

We ran past the school and headed further north.

The sirens faded.

But my heartbeat never seemed to slow down.

CHAPTER 42

What Now?

"Where are we going?" Val asked as she continued to hold my hand. It was getting dark, and I knew we would get cold even in our warm jackets. We needed to find a place to stay.

"I don't know." I was still too shocked to think clearly. Val was older than me, and yet she looked to me to guide her. "I was hoping you would know."

As the cool night air started to ease my nerves, I felt strange holding her hand. I started to let go, but she held on. So I didn't try again. We passed several neighborhoods where I had never really been.

We must have walked twenty blocks before the neighborhood opened up into a shopping and restaurant district. Bright lights flooded parking lots. I looked at my phone and saw it was eight o'clock. The restaurants still had people busy finishing their dinners.

My stomach growled. "You want to eat?"

Val nodded. "You got money?"

I smiled. "Yeah, and so do you." She checked her pocket and found several twenties and a couple of hundreds. I had a little more in mine.

"Where did you get this?" She raised her voice and her eyes narrowed.

"Where do you think?" I couldn't believe she was getting pissed.

"BB's going to be so," she started. Then reality set in. BB was dead, and the money was going to be found. She looked at her handfuls of cash again. She spoke more softly. "I wish you'd taken it all. The police will take it."

I knew what she was saying. But my gut had held me back from taking more than enough to get by until I knew my next move. Despair started to show on Val's face. I squeezed her hand. "You'll be all right."

"You think?" She looked into my eyes. There was something there that scared me. She spoke the words I feared she was thinking. "As long as I've got you."

I pulled my hand away from hers. I stepped back. "Listen, Val. I can't take care of you."

Her beautiful lips and long dark hair came in close. She was shaking. "Please, TJ. Pretend. Just for now. I can't bear being alone. Not right now." I let her put her head on my shoulder. I guessed she was still in shock.

I sighed. "Let's get some food." I took her hand, and we went into Taco Bell.

I wasn't spending more money than I needed to.

I went into the bathroom and pulled the money out of my pockets. I checked my exact amount. Three hundred and twenty dollars were tucked away in my jacket. That wasn't much, but it would hold me for a week. Maybe a few weeks.

When I returned to the table, Val's look had changed. I could see the old Val returning. It was like she was forcing the thought of BB's death away. She was hardening herself. I knew the look. She asked me, "Are you going to lead us now?"

"*What*?" The question surprised me. I hadn't thought for one minute about any of the remaining gang members. Kaden and Brian were dealing with the police, and Bull Dog and the rest of the guys seemed more loyal to their partying than to BB. Why would I want to lead them? I was the youngest one.

"BB always said you'd be the next leader if anything happened to him." Her voice was strong now. Almost too strong. It was the Val I knew who earned her chain. Her chain that was longer than mine.

"I'm too young, and my chain is still only half way around my wrist." I pulled up my jacket sleeve to reveal six small links. It looked like someone had forgotten to complete the tattoo.

Val leaned back in her chair and started laughing. She started laughing so hard that people started staring.

"Shh, people are looking at us." I calmed her down. She wiped her eyes and sighed. We walked outside to a small concrete table that was set off to the side of the parking lot.

I walked around to sit on the bench opposite Val. But it was covered with old gum, so I came back around and sat down next to her. She was finally calm. "BB's

chain was as short as yours when he started. I guess he thought you'd be just like
him. He was so blind. I was so blind. I
thought BB knew everything. I thought he
knew what he was talking about. I thought
you were all he said you were. Tough.
Strong. Fearless."

"You say that like it's a bad thing." I
noticed Val didn't want to hold my hand
anymore.

"He was wrong you know." She looked
at me. The hardness was there. I sat up tall.
I could take what she was ready to give.
"He treated you like he was protecting
you." She looked out over the half-empty
parking lot.

"What are you talking about?" I scooted
away from her. Just a little.

She kept looking at the parking lot. "He
let you stay even though you really never
fit in. Look at you. You never got high. He

always sent you on the easy drops." Then she suddenly looked at me and pulled in close. Her lips were almost touching mine. "You never screwed one of us either." I held her gaze. She stared. I stared. I knew she was wrong about one thing. I was strong. Nothing she said could get to me.

But it wasn't what she said. It was what she did next. Her hand came up to my head and pulled me in for a hard kiss. It took me by surprise. Her lips were hard against mine. I grabbed her hand and jerked it way. I cussed. Her face moved away from mine. But her eyes stayed locked. She was searching. I was frowning. I could feel my anger rise. She finally asked, "What is it with you?"

I shook my head. I knew what it was, but I wasn't telling her. I knew that I still held on to the little redhead who had taught me to dream. I broke my eye contact, held my temper, and got back to business. "I think we should go back. At least to our own homes."

"I don't have one," she said. "But I do have some friends who would let me crash."

We stood and started walking back the way we'd come. We were silent the whole time. Before we reached North High, Val stopped in front of an old apartment building. "My friend lives here." She started to head for the door but turned back around. "TJ?"

"Yeah?" I watched Val's face change.

She tried to smile, but it wasn't easy. "I'm not going to see you again, am I?"

I smiled back. "I sure hope not." She nodded and turned to go.

At the next corner I dropped the cell phone BB gave me into a trash can.

I never saw Val again.

CHAPTER 43

The Box

It was midnight before I opened the door to my apartment. It was the first time I could remember that I felt some relief. The familiar smells relaxed my whole body. I was suddenly so tired.

I pushed open my bedroom door and flipped on my light. An old cornflakes box was on my bed. I frowned and walked up to it. I picked it up. It was heavier than a normal box full of cereal.

"I hoped you would come back." Mom's voice came from behind me. She didn't touch me. She didn't know how. "I kept some things for you while you were gone." She nodded at the box.

I opened it and pulled out Mae's Barbie doll. It was cleaned up and smiling at me. Then I reached into the box and pulled out a handful of letters. The smell of strawberry flooded my whole body. I stumbled to my bed as tears started to flow.

Mom came up to me and patted my shoulder. "Whatever you choose I won't stop you." She reached down, kissed the top of my head, and left. I couldn't remember my mother ever kissing me before. The moment was too much for me. I curled up on the bed with my shoes and jacket still on.

I opened the letters and read. Annabelle started by writing about her daily life, including more time with Kelly and the rest of her new friends. But as the letters continued, her words showed worry and fear for me. She always ended with how much she loved me. Her last letter hurt. She couldn't understand my silence. It must mean I'd moved on. As much as she didn't want to, she would try to move on too. Strong strawberry scent on this last letter gave away the many kisses with which she sealed her last words.

I finally let myself fall into a fitful sleep. The day had been too much.

CHAPTER 44

Opportunity

The metro is only a couple of blocks away."
Billy's voice surprised me as I stood inside
the Texaco convenience store.

I looked to my left and saw Billy
standing behind the cash register. We were
alone. "What?" I walked up to him with
a small jug of milk. I pulled out a twenty
and handed it to him.

He took it and said, "The metro. You
know, the subway."

"I know what the metro is!" I argued
with him, although I wasn't sure why.

"Then why did you say *what*?" Billy
was handing me change.

"Because I'm not sure why you're telling me where the metro is. I've lived here my whole life!" I took the change and shoved it in my back pocket.

"No, you haven't." Billy smiled. He tilted his head slightly. Like he was thinking. "If I remember right, you were gone. And during that time something happened." He looked at me. "A different TJ came home." I just listened. I was drawn to his words. When he saw I was still listening he continued. "I don't know why you were left standing last week. I don't know why you ever joined the gang. But I can tell you this. I was wrong. You have changed. I saw it in your look when they beat up the Pit Bull at school. You didn't like what you saw. At that moment I knew you were putting on the whole thing. You did a damn good job too. You had me believing you were a ruthless gang member."

I kept eye contact. When he paused I asked, "Billy, why are you telling me all this?"

The door opened and a customer walked in. I stepped to the side and waited. I waited for Billy. I waited to hear words I hoped would be true. The customer paid and Billy thanked him. When the door closed again, Billy came around the counter and stood next to me. He was still taller than I was, so I found myself looking up at him.

"The way I see it, you have an opportunity." He crossed his arms. "You can wait until the gang gets back together, or you can get out of here." He looked down on me and smiled. "Don't waste your life trying to become someone you're not."

I shifted the milk to my other hand. "Why are you helping me?" I was confused.

"Because," he smiled as he watched another customer drive up. "Some people are born naturally nice." Then he laughed. I felt an emotion I hadn't felt in a long time. The laughter climbed out of my belly like a caged animal. We both laughed. Together.

The new customer walked in and smiled. Billy went back around the counter and let the man pay. I waited again. I didn't want to leave.

Once the man was gone, Billy leaned over the counter. "Listen, TJ. Go."

"Where?" I asked my heart already racing.

"Don't ask me. You already know." Billy was serious.

As a new customer drove up, I reached out my hand to Billy. "Thanks." He took my hand and I held his. "I am sorry for how I treated you when we were kids."

Billy squeezed my hand hard. "I know."

CHAPTER 45

Unchained

I had it all wrong. I thought I was weak. I thought I wasn't making choices. But I was strong, and I'd made choices and held to them. Val called the choices weak. But I knew I'd been strong. Billy was right. I'd changed. As hard as I tried, I never was much of a Hillside Viper. I knew I could rebuild the gang, but I wasn't about to put myself in that same position again. I had an opportunity. BB was dead. Kaden and Brian had their own worries. It would take some time before the Hillside Vipers would return.

I walked into our small living room. Mom was sitting on the couch. Awake. There were no drugs. The TV was on. Mom had pulled her hair back into two tight braids. She looked at me as I stood in the door. I had the small suitcase I'd gotten from Miss Dixie in my hand.

Mom stood. She walked up to me and for the first time took me in her arms. She cried. I awkwardly lifted my free arm to wrap around her. She whispered, "I'm proud of you." She took my face in her hand and said, "Don't forget me when you make something of yourself." I nodded.

She walked back to the couch and sat down again. She stared at the TV. I knew then what my mother meant when she said she wouldn't stop me. Miss Miller's words came flooding back too. "I promise you I won't get in your way," she'd said.

I stood for a moment longer knowing I was free to go. I was free for the first time.

I finally said, "Mom, you know I love you. I always have."

She turned her head and nodded. "I know, baby. I know."

Then I left.

I walked past the Texaco and kept going for two more blocks down.

I followed the arrow that read Metro.

CHAPTER 46

Home Again

The house was locked. My heart sank. I didn't know what I was expecting. I guess I wanted them all to come flying out the door and embrace me. But no. They must have gone on an afternoon road trip.

I put my suitcase down on the front porch and slowly walked to the bridge. I could feel the promise of spring in the air. I sat in Annabelle's old spot and let my legs swing back and forth.

I thought about school. I'd missed all of last semester, and now I'd gone two weeks without going back to school. I wondered if South High would even take me back. I hoped they would. It wouldn't be easy, but that was nothing new to me.

My fingers felt something carved on the worn wood. I looked down and saw a small heart with *A & TJ* in the middle. There was a huge *X* scratched through my name. I smiled. I knew I deserved it.

I found myself drifting off as I let the spring sun warm my body.

"Wake up, TJ." Mae's sweet face was looking down on me. A little white boy was standing next to her. His black hair looked like someone had cut it using a bowl to shape the edges. I looked at the two of them for a minute before I grabbed Mae and hugged her while she squealed. I stood up with her still under my arm. She waved at the boy. "See, Jack. I told you TJ is a big teddy bear." She looked up at me as her feet kept trying to touch the ground. "TJ, this is Jack. He's new here."

I put Mae down and held my fist out to the young boy. "What's up, Jack?" He carefully tried to tap the top of my fist with his small fist.

I looked up from the two small kids and let my eyes focus on the porch. A red-haired girl was standing still on the top step. She was staring as Miss Dixie came waddling down to the pond. The big woman was waving her arms in the air, and she was yelling, "Oh, TJ! Oh, TJ!" I left the little kids and ran up to throw my arms around my foster mother. She smelled like fresh baked bread.

"I'm home, Miss Dixie. If you'll let me stay." I looked at her. Thankful I was having the homecoming after all.

She kissed my face ten times before she spoke. "Oh, honey! You know you can stay with me for as long as you want." She nudged me. "Miss Miller called and said this might happen." I looked surprised. "We won't get money for you." She laughed and patted my back. "But I don't care. Prince has got a good job and is working evenings while he goes to college during the day. The extra money will help."

"But I can help," I began.

"Let's not talk about it now." She hugged me again and looped her arm into mine pulling me toward the house.

I saw Annabelle awkwardly look down at her feet and then up again. My heart raced. I wasn't sure how she felt. Was she so angry she wouldn't talk to me? But she was standing there looking and then trying not to look. Miss Dixie giggled, "I think Annabelle is happy you're home too."

"I don't know," I said as I watched her suddenly run into the house.

"Give her time, TJ." She patted my arm and added, "You know how she is."

I walked through the front door and noticed nothing had changed. Jack had taken Rico's old room, which left me with my old room. I unpacked my suitcase. I took Mae's Barbie and climbed onto my old bed. I gently placed her on the window sill. She was still smiling at me. I laughed and fell back to stretch out on my bed.

I let my body relax. It must have been a half hour before I was startled by noise. I turned my head.

"So you want to go to the bridge before it gets too cold?" Annabelle had shoved open my door. I sat up on the bed.

I smiled and crossed my arms. "What do you think you're doing? My door was closed," I teased.

She had on blue jeans and a tight sweater. She leaned against the doorway with her arms crossed. "Well, it seems to me you need someone to show you the neighborhood." She just stood there. "Are you coming or not?"

I stood up and walked up close to her. She didn't move. My nose touched the top of her hair, and I let the smell of strawberries fill me. "Yeah. I'm coming. On one condition."

I lifted her chin, and I could see tears begin to fall. She whispered, "And what would that be?"

"I want you to know I never moved on. But I was wrong to try to push you and this place away. I should have called. Well at least said something when I called."

Her eyes got big. "So that was you?"

I smiled. "Can you forgive me?" She leaned into me and kissed me. I kissed back. "I guess that's a yes," I laughed.

I took her hand. She looked down and touched the small tattoo. The tattoo looked like a broken chain to me. Not an unfinished one. I knew I would have it my whole life. I sighed, "It's a long story."

We walked to the bridge and dangled our legs over the water.

The sun was starting to set. We stayed out on the bridge and talked until the cold chased us back indoors. Back to my place at the dinner table with Miss Dixie and all her children. Back to saying a prayer before dinner. Back to holding Annabelle's hand. Back home.